M000295884

# FREE TO PROTECT

TRACEY JERALD

# FREE TO PROTECT

Free to Protect

Copyright © 2022 by Tracey Jerald

No part of this book may be reproduced or transmitted in any form or by any means, electronic or mechanical, including photocopying, recording, or by any information storage and retrieval system without the written permission of the author, except for the use of brief quotations in a review.

This book is a work of fiction. Names, characters, places, and incidents are either products of the author's imagination or are used fictitiously. Any resemblance to actual persons, living or dead, events, or locales is entirely coincidental. The author acknowledges the trademarked status and trademark owners of various products referenced in this work of fiction, which have been used without permission. The publication/use of these trademarks is not authorized, associated with, or sponsored by the trademark owners.

Tracey Jerald

101 Marketside Avenue, Suite 404-205

Ponte Vedra, FL, 3208

https://www.traceyjerald.com


Book Layout © 2017 BookDesignTemplates.com

Free to Protect/ Tracey Jerald

ISBN: 978-1-7358129-6-0 (eBook)

ISBN: 978-1-7358129-5-3(Paperback)

Library of Congress Control Number:TBD

Editor: Missy Borucki

Proof Edits: Comma Sutra Editorial (https://www.facebook.com/CommaSutraEditorial)

Cover Design: Amy Queau – QDesign (https://www.qcoverdesign.com)

978-1-7358129-5-3

❀ Created with Vellum

*To anyone who has ever felt the kiss of fire against their hands or in their hearts.*
*And to my people for pulling me out of the smoke and flames this past holiday season.*

*You know who you are.*
*I love each and every one of you.*

# ALSO BY TRACEY JERALD

## MIDAS SERIES

Perfect Proposal

Perfect Assumption

Perfect Composition

Perfect Order

Perfect Satisfaction (Coming in 2022)

## AMARYLLIS SERIES

Free to Dream

Free to Run

Free to Rejoice

Free to Breathe

Free to Believe

Free to Live

Free to Dance

Free to Wish

Free to Protect

Free to Reunite (Summer 2022)

## GLACIER ADVENTURE SERIES

Return by Air

Return by Land

Return by Sea

## Devotion Series

Ripple Effect

Flood Tide (Coming Spring 2022)

## Standalones

Close Match

Unconditionally With Me-A With Me in Seattle Novella

Go to https://www.traceyjerald.com for all buy links!

# PLAYLIST

Adele: "Hello"
Luke Bryan, Karen Fairchild: "Home Alone Tonight"
Bruce Hornsby, The Range "Set Me in Motion"
Imagine Dragons: "Thunder"
O.A.R: "Peace"
Alessia Cara: "Scars To Your Beautiful"
Howard Jones: "No One Is to Blame"
Delta Rae: "Stronger Than A Lion"
Shawn Mendes: "Use Somebody"
Indigo Girls: "Love's Recovery"
Bruce Hornsby, The Range: "The Show Goes On"
Michelle Branch: "Breathe"

# THE LEGEND OF AMARYLLIS

There are variations regarding the legend of how amaryllis flowers came to be. Generally, the tale is told like this:

Amaryllis, a shy nymph, fell deeply in love with Alteo, a shepherd with great strength and beauty, but her love was not returned. He was too obsessed with his gardens to pay much attention to her. Amaryllis hoped to win Alteo over by giving him the one thing he wanted most, a flower so unique it had never existed in the world before. She sought advice from the oracle Delphi, and carefully followed his instructions. She dressed in white, and for thirty nights, appeared on Alteo's doorstep, piercing her heart with a golden arrow. When Alteo finally opened his eyes to what was before him, he saw only a striking crimson flower that sprung from the blood of Amaryllis's heart.

It's not surprising the amaryllis has come to be the symbol of pride, determination, and radiant beauty. What's also not surprising is somehow, someway, we all bleed a little bit while we're falling in love.

# PROLOGUE

## BRETT

One Year Earlier

"Grace, let's go. We'll drop you at lacrosse on the way to the wedding," Holly calls to my goddaughter from the front door of the house where she and her husband live. I'm comfortable here amid the black-and-white photos that line the walls with family memories. I've been best friends with Holly's husband since we were old enough to understand the concept.

I bark out a laugh at Holly's frustration with her oldest, who can't do anything without it becoming a grand production—even getting to practice on time. Holly's golden-brown eyes narrow in my direction. "Do you want to try to corral her?"

My lips curve. "If it were up to me, I'd just toss her over my shoulder and throw her into the back of the truck, whether she was ready or not."

"Joe's done that on more than one occasion," she admits while casting me the smile that's brought my best friend back to life. I owe the woman in front of me more than I can ever repay. If corralling her perpetually late daughter to practice is what she needs, then I'm all in.

"Hell, Holly, just give me the word," I begin. But just as I'm about to volunteer the services I've honed for close to twenty years, Grace dashes past her stepmother shrieking, "I'm not dressed."

"So, I noticed. You have five minutes before the Bianco Bus leaves without you," Holly returns.

Grace turns and as she streaks by, she quickly plants a kiss on the cheek of the woman who raised her from the time she was a toddler. "Thanks, Mama."

As always, when Grace calls her that, Holly's face transforms into something captivating. I twist my head aside to give them that moment, lifting the bottle of water I've been nursing to my lips in an attempt to swallow down the envy that crawls up and threatens to strangle me.

Closing in on forty, I still haven't found the kind of love that would somehow heal the kiss of the flame that Joe has managed to—not once, but twice. Occasionally I can't help but wonder if I met the person I was supposed to love for eternity and I just didn't recognize them. What a damn shame that would be, I think bitterly.

"What's wrong?" Joe asks, strolling into the room dressed for work. His car is in the shop for some minor repairs, so I offered to pick him up.

"Nothing," I answer immediately.

Even as he pulls his wife into his arms and nuzzles her fiery red hair, he calls me out. "Bullshit. You just made the same face as that time we dared you to drink the homemade sour mix Brady brought in."

Both of us laugh roughly, our amusement laced with the pain of losing our friend and fellow fireman Justin Brady to a fire not long before Joe and Holly got together. Even from a distance between us, I see how Joe's shirt wrinkles when Holly's arms tighten around him.

We are thankful for our memories, unable to do anything but live with them. But the bad ones sure as hell would be easier to handle with someone to love by my side. After consoling his wife, Joe's penetrating blue stare lances through me. Finally, I admit, "I was feeling sorry for myself about how I don't have someone in my life as special as Holly is to you."

Holly's skin flushes as she reaches up, pressing her lips to Joe's before whispering, "Be safe."

"Always am. Drive carefully with the kids," he returns.

She nods. Instead of moving out of the room and yelling for Grace, she makes her way over to me. As is her ritual, she cups the side of my cheek and reminds me, "Be careful, Brett. You're a huge part of this family."

"You got it, Hols," I reassure her with a quick wink for good measure. But the moment she leaves the room, shouting for her daughter to get her butt in gear, my mood plummets.

"A miracle," Joe informs me. "That's what you have to be looking for."

"Like there's one of those dancing on every street corner," I throw back sarcastically.

"We're a part of them every single day. We create them when they shouldn't exist. Maybe you should try something new and believe they're meant for you?" he suggests.

A flurry of activity at the front door captures his attention long enough for me to give his words real thought. I've dated all kinds of women, including Holly's sister Emily long before she ever met her husband. What I can't find is that combination of bravery and need, ambition and warmth, and the underlying spark that causes me to ache every moment she's out of my sight. "And how might you suggest one go about locating such a woman?" My voice drips with sarcasm.

Just as he's about to answer, both of our pagers go off. "Shit!" we shout simultaneously. We're not due on shift for another hour, which means whatever is happening to someone's life is bad. Real bad.

And makes the mourning of my love life paltry by comparison.

# BRETT

**O**ne Year Later
    Right now, I could use somebody standing next to me as I absorb the blow being delivered to me by the doctor who has been working on my case—Kell Wheedon. Parroting what he says, I repeat, "Let me get this right. There's nothing else you can do for me?"

"It's truly remarkable the scarring is so minimal, Captain Stewart."

Instead of responding to being told this is what I'm going to look like for the rest of my life, I slide off the examination table and make my way over to the sink as the burn injury specialist prattles on behind me about the impressive progress I've made in regaining motion.

I hear him but can't comprehend the words, as the image of the man I used to be fades from the mirror, and all I see is leathered skin from my shoulder up to my neck. Without turning, I can easily visualize the scars that run down my back—a parting gift from the flames that took advantage of the unnoticed degradation of my turnout gear. It's something that never should have slipped by with our daily inspections, but it did.

And I paid the price.

Dr. Wheedon goes on to say, "Turnout gear is designed to protect you and survive structural firefighting. It doesn't make you invincible."

Internally, I scoff. *No shit.* "I'm the one carrying the scars, Doc. I think I understand that." He jerks up his chin but says nothing else as I stare down at my image to prove I can. Because if I can't look myself in the eye, how in the hell do I expect others to? Eventually, I turn around and ask, "Mobility?"

"I'd like you to continue physical therapy for at least another month, Captain," he declares.

My lips part in surprise. "I thought you just said there was nothing else you could do."

"Nothing I can do about the appearance of the scars," he corrects. "But I presume, like your colleague, you have a desire to return to your job?"

I nod sharply. I have a war to wage over the beast that did this to me. I won't be able to settle until I do.

"Then you need at least another month of therapy. I don't need to remind you of the peak physical condition people in your profession need to be in to perform their duties."

"And I'm not at it," I acknowledge.

"Close, but not quite." Something changes in Dr. Wheedon's tone. "It's another month, Brett. You'll be ready—both mentally and physically—to resume your duties. I'm certain of it."

I face the mirror again and stare at the scar that rides up the right side of my neck. A scar I got because I was careless. I lift my hand and drag my fingers over the healthy skin before it rides over the harder skin where the scar begins. *Will I be ready?* I question not for the first time. I don't voice that thought. Instead, I smirk and say, "That's all I needed to hear, Doc. You'll send this info over to Chief?"

Concern settles over his face. "Of course. Brett—"

Knowing what's coming, I interrupt, "I used up all my visits with the shrink, Doc." Not that they did much good if the way I wake up sweating in my bed each night is any indication.

"I'm certain they can work something out," he persists.

"I hope I can—for someone who needs it," I tack on. I grab my shirt and haul it over my head. "Are we through here?"

He lets out a beleaguered sigh. "For now. I'll see you back in a month for your final clearance."

I toss him a salute before making my way to the door. Dr. Wheedon calls out my name, causing me to pause and glance over my injured shoulder. Mentally, I high-five myself. *That's something I couldn't have done a year ago.*

"Give the extra therapy some thought. It can help keep your head straight when you need to be someone's hero," he concludes.

I narrow my eyes briefly before informing him, "The only thing I need to have in my mind when I'm back in the suit is what I have to do to conquer the demon in front of me, not the ones that might float about in my head."

"Then you admit you have them." He pounces on my words faster than a spark hitting gasoline.

I ignore them in favor of my primary agenda—to get back to work as fast as possible. "Next month, Dr. Wheedon." I rap my knuckles on the doorframe before opening the door and passing through it.

On the other side, I let out a relieved sigh. Just one more month and I can get back to work.

L ater that night, I decide I'm going to call Dr. Wheedon for the telephone number to the shrink—for my baby sister. *Either that or the nearest priest for an exorcism.* "Jesus, Mel. Tone it down!" I finally shout over her screeching.

"I can't believe you, Brett!"

"What? That I want to get back to living?" I'm incredulous.

"No! That you want to try to die again. Didn't this"—she gestures to my neck and chest—"give you any sort of indication it was time to give it up and get a different job?"

"Are you for real right now? What the hell did I just go through therapy for if not to go back to work?"

"Not to throw it all away," she counters.

Melissa walks straight to me and cups her hand on the side of my neck. I immediately stiffen, not because I can feel her touch, but because of the play of emotions racing across her face: rage, fear, angst. My head drops and I start to confess my fears when her next words dry the words up in my mouth. She whispers, "I can't bear to lose you the way we all lost Justin."

I reach up and grip her wrist firmly. For just a moment, our eyes lock and that's when I realize my sister never got over the overly romanticized crush she had on one of my best friends, who died almost a decade ago when the ceiling of a burning house caved in on him. I tread carefully. "Mel, we've discussed this. Justin and you, it was never going to happen."

She sniffs, disregarding my words yet again. I press on. "He thought of you like a kid sister. You know this."

"That doesn't change how I felt!" She jerks her wrist away and moves back a step.

"It might not, but that's the reality. Just like my going back to work is," I inform her.

"It's the biggest mistake you'll ever make in your life, Brett," she declares dramatically.

"I really don't have the patience for this." Wearily, I rub my hand over my eyes. "I told you because I didn't want it to be a surprise, not because I'm seeking your approval. Hell, I'm almost forty years old. I've been making my own decisions for a long time."

"Look in the mirror, big brother. Time to rethink your strategy because they're apparently the wrong ones," she flings back carelessly.

"Get out of my house." The words escape my lips before I can hold them back.

Her face turns chalk white. "I didn't mean that."

I bite back the *"Are you sure?"* I want to let escape. But I let it slide, knowing where it stems from. Everyone has always spoiled Melissa, who's seven years younger than me—starting with our parents. They pampered and sheltered her from the realities of my father's job—a fireman just like me. By the time she graduated from high school, my dad was already planning to retire to Florida. She wasn't old enough to remember the nights of staying up worrying with Mom or the way Dad would swoop in and kiss them both, still smelling like smoke. Living in her own little world, she never associated my being a fire-fighter with death until Justin.

Now, between Justin and my own close call last year, it's all she can associate with my job—death. But I can't let my baby sister dictate my decisions. Her fear isn't something I can let in, otherwise I might as well walk straight into the flames without wearing the suit. I try to reason with her. "Mel, if I asked you to stop being an interior designer because you work with people I find suspicious, would you?"

Her expression is almost comical. "Of course not! It's my passion. I live for being able to . . ." Her words trail off as she puts together what I'm trying to say. She swallows hard. "I'm scared, Brett. I'm so scared for you."

I hold my arms open and she dashes right into them. I bury my face in her hair and inhale the sweet smell I took for granted when she was a baby. It's something I never really understood until I lived my life inhaling smoke day in and day out. I murmur, "It will be all right."

She lifts a tear-streaked face. "How do you know?"

"Because I'm your brother and I said so," I declare authoritatively.

She gives a hiccuping laugh before stepping back. "Have you regained your full memory of what happened?"

I shake my head before I roam over to the kitchen to finish preparing our dinner. "No. I recall Joe and I went into the building and toward the kitchen because we heard some people might still be inside. After that, the next thing I remember is the heat. Why?"

Melissa hesitates. "I'm sure there's more to the story."

"If there is, I need to remember it on my own. You know what the doctor said," I remind her firmly.

Her cheeks flag with bright red slashes. She flings out, "I don't see why it matters at this point."

"And that's not up for you to decide, Mel. It's up to the experts." And something we'll be discussing with the chief when Joe and I present to him our fit for duty certificates next month. I'm more impatient for those gaps of time to be erased than anyone, apart from Joe.

She opens her mouth to contradict me, but I cut her off. "The subject is closed. Now, tell me what new house you're working on."

It's a warning—I have no desire to further this conversation with her. Fortunately, my sister heeds it. "It's one of the enormous ginger-breads on Main Street," she begins.

Good. This is good. I can listen to Melissa meander on about decorating while internally I struggle with one of the questions she asked.

Can I operate at my best if I don't know what took me down?

# JILLIAN

*It's a beautiful morning in Collyer, Connecticut. Expect the spring weather to hold for the next several days. There's no need for coats.*

I half-listen to the news playing on the television as I stare at the contents of my closet. I'm feeling more like myself today. For the first time in a year, I decide I'm ready to smile again and shove the fear where it belongs—in the past.

Pulling a yellow sweater I crocheted in a loose pattern over a tank, I declare, "No more. That damn bitch doesn't get one more day of my life. Last night was it. I'm taking charge." I squeeze my hands into fists at my side. At least, I try to. The physical therapist reassured me it would take just a little more time to regain the last bit of motor function. "But you'll get it back, Jillian. You've far surpassed what I expected you would."

"That's fantastic," I told her. But while my wounds have mostly healed, I know of a few people whose haven't and they're never far from my mind. After my last physical therapy session, I recognize I have no reason to feel sorry for myself. I'm alive—and not just physically. It's why, after a trip to visit my grandmother in the assisted living facility and some time with my psychologist, I've decided to stop guarding myself the way I have been.

Grabbing my purse, I head down the stairs and embrace the magnificent spring day. The second I step outdoors, the wind lifts my hair and brushes against my skin in between the knit. I lift my face to feel the kiss of the cool breeze against my cheek, my neck, appreciating the simple pleasure for what it is.

A second chance at life.

Immediately, I turn left and fall back into the routine I so abruptly abandoned with ease. My apartment is conveniently located down the street from the most delicious reason to pull myself together and escape the self-imposed isolation of my home—the Coffee Shop. Owned by Matt and Ava Barlow, the aroma of their renowned coffee lures me in like a hungry catfish taunted with chicken livers. I'm hooked from a half a block away and being reeled in fast. I'm jogging by the time I reach the door.

My hands slapping against it cause the bells to tinkle merrily, alerting Ava. She rushes over, her arms wide open. "Jilly! Honey, it's so good to see your face in here." And within seconds, the warmth of acceptance I feel in her embrace makes me believe my scars could be very well eliminated by the sheer power of a hug, leaving the wounds in the past where I'm determined they should remain.

Resting my head upon her shoulder, I murmur, "You too. I'm—"

"Don't you dare say you're sorry," she interrupts, scolding me.

"I should have been able to come to you."

"Kelsey let us know how you were. Matt had to practically sit on me to keep from checking on you after you came home from the hospital."

I bite my lip imagining Ava's burly husband performing such an act. She plows on. "He said healing occurs in stages and you'd come back when you were ready."

"Matt's a wise man."

"You weren't ready then, but now you are. It's as simple as that." She pulls back and searches my face.

My cheeks lift as I give her a full-blown smile. "I'm ready to try. That has to count for something."

She squeezes my upper arms before letting me go and pointing to a tiny two-person booth in the back corner nearest to the kitchen. "I'll bring your macchiato over. As you can see, nothing much has changed. She's completely engrossed in a scene—it might take her a while to emerge. Who knows what condition she'll be in."

I can't prevent the giggle. "And that's any different how?"

Ava sighs. "It's not. I hope you brought something to occupy yourself. Kelsey might be awhile. If not, you're welcome to hang out with me and Matt."

I pat my purse. "I'm working on a new piece for the store."

Her eyes widen. "You are?"

I nod. Her eyes water. Before I can do anything, she reaches into her apron and yanks out a napkin to dab at them. "You really are better, aren't you?"

"I'm better, not perfect."

"None of us are, darling. Now, shoo. I'll be right there with your drink." Ava scuttles off, leaving me to make my way to the back corner of the smallish café.

Sliding into the booth across from the friend I made when she'd visited her cousin Ava many summers earlier—long before she became the world-renowned author, Kee Long—I take stock of the way Kelsey's fingers are flying across her laptop keyboard furiously. "Ava wasn't kidding," I murmur. I dig in my purse, wincing as the corner of my wallet grazes the sensitive palm of my right hand. Finding my phone, I pull it out and snap a picture to send to Ava later. She doesn't even bat an eye, so caught up in her newest novel.

Slipping back into our routine disrupted by the tragedy that affected so many Collyer residents a year earlier, I pull out my knitting. The dark gray cashmere called to me when I was ordering from the supplier—the stormy color speaking to me like a story. *Maybe that's because it's the only thing you could see, feel, touch,* I ponder.

Ava delivers my drink and steps back to observe me for a few moments as I carefully manipulate the yarn, despite how much slower the fingers of my right hand work the strand over the needle. Pausing, I take a sip of the tantalizing brew before starting on the next row. *If I pretend, I could imagine it's just like before the fire.* The insidious thought pops into my mind. Except, as the silky yarn grazes over the tips of my healed fingers, it's different. Before, there were some mornings where I'd leave my thriving business to take a break with Kelsey. Others, I'd skip because I knew I'd be visiting my grandmother later in the day.

That day was one of them.

My stomach churns frantically as I recall how it all turned on a dime. It was a day as beautiful as this one . . .

*Her nose sniffs the air like a bloodhound. "Well, how about we go out to lunch? Pierre burned the stew. Again."*

*"Gran, how can you possibly know that?" I laugh as my grandmother besmirches the cook at the facility on the outskirts of Collyer.*

*"Because it smells like branded cattle," she declares.*

*"And you know what that smells like through experience?" I challenged.*

*"Listen, child. You'd be surprised at the things . . ."*

"Jill? Jilly? Are you all right?" Kelsey lays her hands over mine. Her gray eyes are concerned.

I open my mouth to spew platitudes, but before I can say a word, she declares, "Don't tell me you are fine."

My fingers crumple the fine yarn beneath them. It's too bad the tip of one finger can only feel the bite of the yarn pull against my skin. "No, but I will be. That's what this is all about."

Eyes that understand too much stare back at me for a long moment. Then she relaxes back in her seat, still not letting go of my hands. "It's good to have you back."

"I didn't really go anywhere," I say, though we both know that's a lie. I went somewhere few people can get to. To get there, you have to pass through a fog where night and day are visually indistinguishable. The cloud rises so quickly your mind, your soul gets twisted. To say nothing of the damage your body suffers along the journey.

"Right. And I suddenly lost thirty pounds."

Without thinking, I reach across the table and whack Kelsey in the arm with my damaged hand.

"Ow," she moans. "Is it just me, or do you hit harder now?"

Calm as you please, I reach for my coffee and take a sip. "You deserved it. And there's got to be some fringe benefit to not having feeling in my fingers."

Her eyes flash with a multitude of feelings: fear, desperation, and finally, gratitude. "I'll take it. Just to have you sitting across from me."

A rush of emotions swirls through me. But I leave it with a simple, "Same. Now, tell me about what's going on with your new book. This blanket isn't going to knit itself."

"Right." With that, I spend the rest of the morning taking another step toward healing.

# BRETT

One Month Later

"Hey, Chief, do you have a minute?" Joe and I roll our eyes as yet another probie calls out to Joe's father. We've been trying to have a conversation in his office for the last hour to convince him we're fit to return to full-time active duty. He's had our physical reports for days and we're both stuck behind desks, which is driving us insane.

"Give me a five, Hoffman. Can't you see I'm in the middle of something?" Joseph Bianco, Senior, known to all around Collyer as "Chief," bellows back. He mutters, "I'm tempted to demand that kid buy himself a clue along with some air freshener for his boots. His damn feet stink up the entire place. We need an alarm—some kind of early warning signal made by Dr. Scholl's."

Joe hides his laugh by coughing into his hand, but I don't even have to try. Humor is the last thing I've experienced since I was kissed by the beast and the bitch walked away victorious. The only thing I give a damn about is proving myself physically fit so I can get back to work to hunt her.

Kill her.

The way she tried to kill me and those I love.

Out of the corner of my eye, I catch sight of the scar that weaves itself up over Joe's arm. I know the scar extends further than that, both up and down—almost as bad as my own. *Because the crazy motherfucker unbuttoned his coat to save you both.* The thought pops into my head out of nowhere, almost knocking me off my feet.

Joe Bianco almost lost his life because he was trying to save mine. He has a wife, kids. *He should have let me burn.* But even though I would never ask my best friend to give up his life for me, the thought of the fire taking more of me than it already did makes me so nauseous, I begin to sweat profusely.

A few months ago, I asked him how he had such a grip on his anger during physical therapy. Joe admitted, "I don't." He glanced around the room before confessing, "If it wasn't for Holly and the kids, I don't know who or what I'd be."

I know the answer. He'd be just like me. But I let him continue to purge his thoughts. "I can't give up. I won't let the bitch get another chance to take those I love from me. I have to do everything I can."

I vividly recall the last time the flames aimed her vengeance at Joe. I wish my motives for being back in the uniform were as altruistic as his, but I just want a shot at payback. "Yeah."

He swallowed before resting his hand against the squishy ball he had been squeezing for the umpteenth time to get the muscles in his fingers to work again. "And she already told me it would kill her if I gave up."

Now, as we sit in front of Chief's desk, I can't help but notice the cluster of photos of Joe, Holly, and their kids displayed with a place of pride. And it makes me more bitter because what woman would want a man as scarred as I am?

No, the fire took more from me than layers of skin. It took my future—the shot I had at love.

. . .

Hours later, we walk out of the brick firehouse still without authorization to go back to full duty. "I want you both to go home and really think if getting back into the gear is what you want," Chief finally yielded.

"There's nothing physically preventing us from doing the job," I snarl as I reach my truck. "I'm sick and tired of being sent out on non-essential calls. How many times can your brother-in-law's cat get stuck in a tree?"

Joe frowns at me. "More than you think. Rebel climbs to the top of cabinets . . . listen, why are we talking about my in-laws? We've been cleared to be back in the house. It's a step. We'll get where we need to be. What's your problem?"

I rub my jaw, my fingertips feeling the hair I started growing to detract from the scars running up my neck. I declare bluntly, "Your father. He's making this decision, not as the chief, but because he's terrified something is going to happen to you."

Joe bristles. "I disagree."

I scoff. "Why am I not surprised?"

"I think he's making this decision because he doesn't want something to happen to either of us, something permanent. To him, it wasn't all that long ago we lost Justin, Brett. There hasn't been another since."

I suck in a deep breath before releasing it slowly. "I hate he's gone. Mel said something similar not too long ago."

"My mother pointed out to me the other night at our family dinner how much this is weighing on my father—not just as my dad, but as chief. He almost lost two more of his people."

"Maybe he should speak with someone at Victim's Assistance," I recommend lamely, knowing it will never happen. Probably because Chief knows the futility of it.

"I'm sure he'll pencil that in. Right after he realizes we're fit for duty." Joe's frustration with me is evident. He storms past to fling open the door to his Explorer. "What do you want to do?"

What he leaves unsaid is *if you're not cleared for duty.* "I don't know.

Honest to God, Joe, I can't think that far ahead. Getting back to work is all I can focus on."

He passes the key fob with incredible dexterity back and forth between his fingers. "Me too. This is all I ever wanted." With those parting words, he slides behind the wheel and slams the door.

*No, you wanted love, and you found it. Twice. Be grateful for that. Do everything in your power to protect it. Not all of us will have that chance.* I think as I watch my best friend peel out of the lot.

For long moments, I stand in the cool spring air and debate what I should do next. Until I realize there is only one thing left to do.

Go home.

# BRETT

I wake up, drenched in sweat, my chest heaving after my nightmare.

Or was my mind finally opening up enough to let the events of that afternoon in, just like the psychologist said it eventually would?

I reach for the bottle of water on the side of the bed, take a large swig, and force myself to recall the events of what happened a year ago.

*When we arrived on the scene, fire trucks and ambulances were everywhere. To an outsider, it likely looked like a circle of chaotic hell with the flames shooting up from one side of the building. After I slammed my truck into park, Joe and I sprinted over to our company engine. "What's the deal, Chief?" I yelled over the cacophony of noise.*

*"Grease fire in the kitchen that went out of control," he shouted back.*

*Joe demanded, "Residents?"*

*"Accounted for and receiving treatment. There are some visitors they're trying to locate in the crowd."*

*"Any inside?" The words were barely out of my mouth when a small disturbance among the residents had a doctor rushing over.*

"No idea. They're trying to put out the fire, but it's an older building."
Meaning if it climbed into the walls, the whole shell could collapse.

"We'll do a quick sweep and see where we're needed," Joe assured his father.

He clapped Joe on the shoulder and gave me a stern look. "Stay cool. Both of you."

I jerked my chin at Joe. "Gear up, buddy."

The two of us darted around the side of the truck and pulled on our turnout gear before breaching the barrier of onlookers to enter the wall of heat.

"Remind me never to put you in a one of these places," I called out to Joe as we swept the first few halls for frightened residents or visitors.

He snorted. "Thanks, buddy. Same goes."

We turned down a hall toward the kitchen and spied the team fighting the mammoth wall of dancing flames. I was about to tell Joe we should shift our priority to help when two things happened.

I tripped over an unconscious body.

And the ceiling collapsed in on me.

"Holy hell. What happened to them?" I whisper in the cocoon of the night.

And did I push hard enough to save them?

The next morning, I drive over to Joe and Holly's to find an all-out battle waging. They don't hear me enter through their back door, their voices are so loud. Grace, who I think is running to me, tries to brush past with tears on her face. I catch her by the elbow. "What's happening?"

"It's like this all the time, Uncle Brett. Ever since the fire, Dad does nothing but turn in on himself. And when Mom tries to pull him out of it . . ." The sound of a door opening and slamming before heavily booted feet stomp around the living room give us both an indication of which parent stormed out of the house. "I have to go."

"Where?" I demand. Joe will kill me if someone doesn't know where his precious Grace is going.

"Just to Kaylie's," she pleads. Kaylie Marshall has been Grace's best friend since she was three. Now a cousin by marriage, her home is walking distance from Joe and Holly's place.

I relent. "Go. I'll handle your father."

She leans up and presses a kiss on my cheek. "Thanks. Love you."

The protective shell around my heart that's as leathered as my skin cracks open just a bit. "Love you too, kid. Now go."

Grace grabs her purse and jacket before dashing out the back. Just as I'm about to make my way through the kitchen, Joe storms in shouting, "Grace? Honey, it was just a spat."

As I reach for a bottle of water from the fully stocked drink cooler, I say, "Apparently a huge one. You drove away your wife and daughter."

Joe's lips curl. "Don't you start. Where's my girl?"

I chug the water before giving him an answer. "At Kaylie's. I figured that was safe enough." I finish the bottle, tossing it in recycling before sticking my nose in his business. "I thought you two were past all the fighting?"

He deflates right in front of me. "We were. Are."

"Obviously," I drawl.

"I hadn't discussed going back to work with Holly until today."

"Are you crazy, Joe?" I ask calmly.

"And that's what she said—how she said it—to set me off," he bites off.

I wave my hand. "Forget the job. This is your wife, man. We three almost bought it. If the backup team hadn't gotten us out . . ."

"Whoa, buddy. Talk about crazy. What do you mean? What three? It was just you and me in there." Joe walks around the fridge and gets his own bottle. Twisting the top off, he takes a swig.

I slowly shake my head. "No. There was the person I tripped over. There were three of us, Joe. There was someone else they pulled out."

He places the bottle on the counter. "So, since there were no deaths, you and I have had each other."

"And they've been alone," I declare grimly.

His face takes on the same cast. "We left someone unprotected."

"Not anymore, we won't," I announce. Now I'm more fired up than ever to get cleared to work so I can protect the people who don't have the ability to when the monster comes knocking. At least then I can justify to myself I've done something worthwhile with the semblance of life I have left.

# JILLIAN

**S**ix Months Later

"Are you paying attention?" my grandmother asks from her rocking chair. The old gingerbread house that was converted to the new assisted living facility on Main Street makes visiting her even more convenient than ever. I fall back in my chair and admire how fast her frail hands move as she crochets an advanced blanket pattern out of a rich magenta-colored yarn I found online called Fairy Tale. "Two of my friends are getting married, so I'm making them blankets for their beds," she informed me primly when I asked her what prompted her to search out such a vibrant color in the first place.

"At your age?" I blurted out.

She sniffed. "Love doesn't recognize age, Jilly."

As my gaze meets hers, I can't help but think, *Good. If true love can have a happily ever after at eighty-six, then there's still hope for me yet.* I merely question, "Are they going on a honeymoon?"

Much to my surprise, Grandma confirms, "The nurses are helping us decorate an unused room."

I groan. "That was a rhetorical question, you know?"

"Then you shouldn't have asked it." Grandma's fingers stop

moving as she stares off dreamily. "It's going to be perfect. We're pushing their beds together so they can hold hands while they sleep."

"That sounds beautiful." And it does. The simple beauty of the image she paints causes a pang of longing deep inside of me. It's just too bad it's not in my future.

I rub the tips of the fingers of my right hand over the skin of my left. Nothing. Part of me wants to weep because after all I've been through, I'll never be able to feel it. I've been reassured time might help to heal some nerves, but I took for granted the sensations I felt before and may never experience again.

My scars are minimal because of the bravery of two of Collyer's firemen throwing their bodies on top of mine. And I owe a debt of gratitude I can never repay for my life. But I feel like I'm stripped naked. So much of what I do involves the sense of touch. *Be grateful you still have feeling in your one hand,* I berate myself as I drop my knitting needles into my lap and drag my left hand over the right one to reassure myself I haven't lost feeling there as well. The psychologist I spent the better part of the year working with reminded me this kind of anxiety was normal with what I endured.

*My life has been spent circling rings of fire. More so than any circus performer,* I think bitterly. Outwardly, I blurt out, "I wish I'd never gone to the kitchen that day. If I hadn't, maybe I'd still feel like me. Maybe I wouldn't lie awake at night speculating about what would have happened if I didn't."

"Jilly." Just my name, but it's said so helplessly my heart aches.

I lift my hands and the bell-sleeved sweater I donned earlier falls back to expose the tattoos I recently added to my wrists to blur the demarcation between where my original skin ends and the leathery-textured skin of the underside of my hands begins. The fluid script with the quotes from *As You Like It* on each wrist where the skin will never match again. "I'm stronger."

"You are, darling." Her smooth-skinned hand comes up to cup my cheek. A small part of me wants to flinch away, but I don't. It's not for me to cause harm to others because my trial by fire was literal.

"I'll never forget, Grandma. That's an impossibility."

"Naturally."

"But I've survived before. I'll do it again," I vow.

I lift my knitting and begin the next row when her soft voice whispers, "And you'll do it beautifully."

I square my shoulders and keep knitting.

Yes, I will. I won't ever disrespect the people who saved me from a burning building not to.

Later that afternoon, I meticulously rub the special moisturizer into my new tattoos. Then I begin the lengthy process of moisturizing my hands. "It's crazy how often I have to do this as the weather has become cooler. It takes forever," I inform Kelsey while she's on speaker.

"Listen, I know you don't want to hear this, but I'm grateful the damage was . . . minimal. The burns were limited to your hands and wrists. It could have been so much worse."

"I know." And I do, which is why I agreed to go as her date to the fundraiser tonight to support Collyer's Police and Fire Departments.

I imagine her shaking her dark head on the other side of the phone as she changes the subject back to the reason behind the call. "What time do you want me to pick you up for our hair appointments?"

Impulsively, I announce, "Now. Let's just drive around until we have to be at Shimmer. I just want to appreciate the beauty of being alive. I was given a second chance and I need not spend it in my apartment."

On the other end of the line, I hear Kelsey's shoes beating out a rapid staccato against her hardwood floors. "I'm leaving in three minutes. I'll be at your front door in less than ten," she warns.

"I'll be downstairs waiting. I promise."

"You'd better!" She laughs just before hanging up.

Hours later, after Gail and her team untangled the mass of knots in our windblown hair, we're back at Kelsey's, searching through her dresses and shoes for something for me to wear. She waves her arm as if to say have at it.

Considering my friend is ridiculously shoe obsessed, I start there, sending up a small prayer of thanks we wear the same size. "Black tie, you said?" I mumble as the scent of leather hits my nostrils.

"Yes. Ever since Amaryllis Events took over the fundraiser years ago, the spring is for the race and the fall is the black-tie ball. Personally, I think that was Em's doing."

"Em?" I question.

"Emily Freeman-Madison. She's one of the family members who founded Amaryllis Events and is the brainchild behind Amaryllis Designs. Wait, I have one that would be perfect for you to wear." I'm shoved to the side as Kelsey dives into the depths of her walk-in.

What she emerges with is a floor-length pleated gown in dove gray. The front comes down to a spectacular *V* almost to the waist. "Wow," I whisper in awe when Kelsey spins the dress on the hanger, and I get a load of the crystals holding the front to the back waist. "You want me to wear this?" Unconsciously, the fingers of my left hand reach to touch those on the right before I let them drop.

That's when she jolts me back to the here and now. "No, I think *you* want to wear it. I'm just giving you the opportunity to before I move." She thrusts the dress back out, mine to leave or take.

And with my right hand, I reach out and clutch the satin-covered hanger with all my might.

# BRETT

I'm standing there in my full-dress uniform when Joe clasps my shoulder. He announces cheerfully, "My wife has abandoned me."

A few months ago, I might be alarmed at the joviality in his statement, but Holly broke through. It's good to know that there's another side to this nightmare for some people. Catching a glimpse of his father approaching, I lift my drink to my lips to hide my smirk before I ask, "Was it because you smell? Because really, you should have showered before you came to this kind of event."

Joe shoves me, almost knocking me into an older couple, both of whom jump. I dip my head before apologizing. "I deeply regret Captain Bianco's boorish manners during such an esteemed event."

Joe's eyes promise retribution as Chief approaches with his wife —Joe's mother—Denise. "Do I need to separate you two?" He's blinking rapidly as he tries to aim a beady-eyed glare at both of us.

"Holly got you with her camera, didn't she?" Joe guesses.

Chief groans, making us all laugh. "I swear, your wife didn't put that thing down during the delivery of our grandchildren, Joe. What on earth made me think she'd leave it home tonight?"

"Give her a break. She's working tonight, Pop. I'm stag."

Maybe it's the highball I've been nursing, but I feel more like myself than I have in ages. Wrapping an arm around Joe's shoulder, I snuggle up to my best friend like I was two and needed to cuddle with my teddy bear.

"Get off me, you ass," Joe laughs.

"And here I was going to offer to be your date," I sigh dramatically.

Everyone in the small group breaks into laughter, causing the ice around my heart to melt a little more. I recall what it was like when I was younger and I clowned around all the time, when laughter was a typical part of my day. Now, there are a million miles between me and the man who felt the world crash in on him—literally. It's no secret those days and that man are buried in the ashes of a building that's being rebuilt.

If only there was something—someone—who gave a damn about me. Sure, there's my family—my parents and my sister. And of course, Joe and his brood. But if I'd found that someone before the fire, maybe I could have been resurrected from the ashes instead of leaving my soul as footprints in the rubble and dust. Maybe I wouldn't feel like I'm drifting on the wind.

Like it's answering me, a gust of wind swirls around us, causing women to lift their hands to their meticulously arranged hairdos. Men turn their backs as the front door opens to admit a late arrival.

Their loss because they don't get a glimpse of the smoke-colored vision that streaks into the room, her dress swirling around her like a Hollywood movie starlet. Dark hair lifts off her neck in a wreath of braids and swaths of messy strands. I swallow hard at the vast amount of creamy skin outlined in a dress that plunges almost to her waist. When she turns to say something to the woman she's with, her cheeks flush—nerves or excitement? I narrow my eyes and catch as her teeth drag over her plump lower lip, enticing me to do the same.

My breath becomes a bit jagged as the two women mingle. Are they together? Friends? Immediately, I become as intrigued as she engages in some small talk with the very recognizable Matt and Ava Barlow. My body jerks forward intuitively toward her, like it has a mind of its own. Acknowledging how much I ache for the sweetness of a woman's touch for the first time since the fire.

"Who is she?" I murmur, entranced as she throws her head back and laughs at something the cantankerous cook mutters. Her surprise is visible from halfway across the ballroom as he catches her hand and spins her out. I become hard as a rock when I glimpse more of her smooth skin through the crystal chains holding up the back of her gown.

Something inside of me is clawing at me to get to her before she escapes. "That woman who just walked in the gray gown—who is she?"

"Who?" Joe lifts his own drink.

My jaw falls a bit. "Gray dress. Just came through the door like she owned the room." *And me or any male she might want in it,* I despair.

Chief stills. He probes, "You don't recognize her?"

I ignore the way Joe's eyes narrow at his father's words. "No. Should I?"

There's a quick flash of something behind Chief's eyes before he informs me, "Her name is Jillian Beale. She's a local business owner."

My eyes narrow as a swarm of people approach the women. "And apparently, a popular one."

Denise explains, "That's likely due to her friend."

*Who cares about her friend?* I'm certain I said the words to myself until Denise beams at me. "How lovely, Brett. Be sure to tell her that. Her friend is Kee Long."

Now it's Joe's jaw that's unhinged. "The bestselling author? The same author I read to my kids?"

"Yes, son. Ava's her cousin," Denise informs him.

"Great. Her friend's an author. Tell me more about Jillian, Mama D." I brush past the author friend to get to the heart of the matter— the woman who stirred something inside me I was certain died in the fire.

Denise glances up at Chief, who shrugs. Helplessly, she adds, "Jillian owns a yarn and craft store beneath her apartment on Main

Street. I know she's single and not dating anyone. Her only living relative is ..."

But I stopped listening after I heard the woman that sparked something back to life inside me is available. I shove my glass at Joe and head in the direction of the growing crowd.

# JILLIAN

Amused, I lean over and whisper to Ava, "Does it ever get old?"

"Watching Kel . . . I mean Kee deal with her fans?" At my nod, she shakes her head. "No. For so long, her life broke my heart. What she went through as a kid was traumatic enough. Her father was an awful human. I'm going to miss her when she moves to New Orleans."

"Me too. But she and Angel have been planning this forever," I remind Ava.

"Lord, heaven help that city. And Darin." Ava names Angel's husband.

"Here, here," I lift an imaginary glass in a toast.

Seconds later, I find a real one in it. I flash a smile at who I assume is Matt but then I freeze.

*It's him.* He holds out his right hand to shake. "Captain Brett Stewart. Collyer Fire Department."

Automatically doing the same, something it takes me a minute to realize I do because I am so disconcerted by Brett's presence. The only thought flashing through my mind is, *He doesn't recognize me.* A part of me is so grateful, and the other feels like this is something I need to clear up and fast. But when he brushes his lips against the back of my hand, I feel the zing that rushes through me at the contact. "Jillian Beale," I respond over the hoopla, awaiting his response.

I don't expect the response to be the sizzle between us intensifying.

Standing next to me, Ava beams at the man who saved my life by throwing his body on top of mine. "Hey, Brett. You clean up well."

Charmingly, he lifts her hand to his lips and bows over it gracefully. "Ava, there are too many mornings I couldn't wake up without you there."

"Excuse me," Matt butts in as his arm slides around his wife's waist.

Brett continues smoothly, "But really, it's Matt being so delectable that does it for me."

I try to hold in my laughter at Matt's outrage, but can't. Laughter erupts freely. I flap a hand in front of my face, uncaring which one it is. After I get myself under control, I apologize. "I'm sorry, but I've been hanging around with Kel . . ."

"Kee," Ava and Matt remind me.

"Right, Kee. I've been hanging around her for too long."

Brett purses his lips. "You don't wake up in the morning with thoughts of Matt between a few slices of toast and a side of hash browns?"

At this point, we're drawing attention with the amount we're giggling. Kelsey extracts herself from her fans and makes it over. "Whatever you're laughing about, I'll take two."

Which sets us off all over again. While we're recovering, Brett slides his fingers beneath my elbow. "Would you like to dance?"

Before I get a chance to answer, Kelsey, Ava, and Matt scatter like rats on a ship. I blink several times to be certain I heard correctly. "Me? You'd like to dance with me?"

A twisted smile crosses his face, intensifying the one bald patch on it where hair doesn't grow. *Because of me.* His words take me out of my own musings and land me back in front of him. And the mix of frustration, sadness, and hurt wafting off him strikes me like a sledge-hammer. "I apologize, Ms. Beale. I forgot for just a moment my place is to protect the citizens of Collyer."

He starts to shift away when I finally string words together in my mind. I primly declare, "Then I can only assume the safest place to be in the room will be with you, Captain Stewart?"

He sucks in a breath so deep I know I'm being pulled toward him with the strength of it. "I'll protect you from everything, Jillian. Even myself."

*You might have to once you realize who I am.* But just like Cinderella, I can allow myself the illusion of dancing in a gorgeous man's arms and hoping maybe he'll call on her the next day. Instead of replying, I just nod at the ridiculously handsome man who life decided to take a bite out of the same day she took one out of me.

A hush seems to descend upon the room as Brett leads me onto the dance floor. With a wry smile, I announce, "It's no secret to anyone you're doing this because you're a good man, Captain."

"Brett. And what makes you say that?" He twirls me in a spin that causes my dress to float out around me.

"Well, Brett, most of Collyer probably considers me to be some-what of a wallflower." He spins us past Holly Freeman-Bianco. The gorgeous photographer lowers her camera for a split second. Behind the lens, her face is a mix of incredulousness and joy, much like I'm certain my own is when I tip my head back and find Brett staring down at me intently. "I rarely do events like this."

"Might I say you're doing this one very well?" He spins me again, and I lose focus on the faces and turn my attention to the only one that matters.

"Much like you dance very well. Lessons?" I question.

He groans and my lips curve into a smile. "My mother. She and Mama D demanded Joe and I take lessons as kids."

"Joe?"

"Bianco," he nods to the side where the fire chief and his son are standing. Instead of the vacant but polite smile I'm normally treated to by both men, one's smile is sad while the other is thoughtful. "Our families have been friends since we were two."

"You mean gorgeous firefighters aren't hatched?" I mutter under my breath. At least I think I do.

"I'm not good looking." What was a friendly, almost flirtatious tone before has turned to steel.

I blink up at him as we've stopped moving on the dance floor. A beautiful blonde comes rushing up. "Brett! I just got here, you dork. You should have picked me up." She wails on his arm.

His lips curve as he drops his arms from around me like I have developed some kind of disease. "I'm sorry, Mel. Jillian, my sister Melissa. Mel, this is Jillian . . ."

"Beale. I know who she is, Brett. I just can't believe you're dancing with her." Melissa's eyes—the same forest green as her brother's—narrow as they land on my face. Then they drop to my hands before they rise. I just hope the burning hatred in her gaze doesn't scald anyone else. After all, I know firsthand how much pain fire can cause when it touches you unexpectedly.

He steps back and his gaze narrows on his sister's. "What the hell are you talking about, Mel?"

Even though I brace for it, nothing could have prepared me for the reaction Brett has to his sister's accusatory tone. "You told me you remembered what happened to you in the fire."

"I did. I do."

Melissa flings her arm at me. "She's the one. She's the reason you were burned."

Brett jerks back, as if I'm suddenly going to burst into flames at will. His "I didn't remember who it was" comes out choked.

Melissa launches at me, like she's planning on striking me. I jerk up my hands to protect my face from any attacks.

It's Brett who pulls them away before declaring, "That's not who I was brought up to be, Mel. Neither were you."

"Brett," she begins.

His fingers brush over the tips of the fingers of my right hand. I only know this because I'm watching them as they draw away. "I was raised to serve and protect. I don't get to choose who, and I don't get to choose when."

With that parting comment, Brett slips an arm around his sister and guides her off the dance floor.

I'm not certain how long I stand there in shock before Kelsey comes up to me. "Are you all right?"

"I'm sorry," I say automatically.

"For what?"

"For bleeding all over your dress."

"You're bleeding?" She spins me in a tight circle to check for any streaks of red.

"That's what it feels like on the inside."

"You never got a chance to tell him?" she asks.

I shake my head. "His sister interrupted."

"What were you going to say to Brett?" a deep male voice interrupts us. I look up and there are the somber blue eyes of Captain Joe Bianco.

"The same thing I need to say to you. I'm sorry. I'm so sorry you both got injured because you had to come in and rescue me." And with that rushed apology, I lift my borrowed dress and race off the dance floor, out into the cool, fall air.

# BRETT

illian Beale. Now I have a name and a face to accompany the nightmares I suffer with night after night. It's an exquisite one, making living in this shell of who I used to be even harder to accept.

Wandering over to the front window, I'm not surprised when I see Joe's car pull up. He doesn't bother knocking, instead just flings the door open. "Are you all right?"

My lips twist and I ask, "Why wouldn't I be?"

"Why indeed? What happened?"

"I had to escape. Going back to the ball was impossible, not with Mel behaving the way she did. Why aren't you still there?" I ask pointedly.

Joe steps by my side. "I told Holly I'd be back. I wanted—no, needed—to make certain you were okay after what you found out."

We've been through everything together, me and Joe. Everything from grammar school all the way through training. Every time the beast tries to take a bite of one of us, the other is at their side. So I feel comfortable blurting the thought that's been running through my mind over and over since I dragged my sister from the fundraiser.

"She's the first woman I've been remotely attracted to since the fire. I saw her and had to be near her. Me." I laugh bitterly.

"And what's wrong with you?" Joe questions.

Answering without words, I reach up and yank down the collar of my dress shirt, exposing the scars that run from my beard to my chest.

Joe pushes up his sleeve, partially exposing the scars he too sustained the afternoon we entered the facility. "So?"

"So, you met your wife before." What I leave unsaid is, *Who would want me like this?*

Ever.

"You're an idiot," he says succinctly.

"Thanks a lot."

"No, I mean it. There was a hell of a lot more to you than just a pretty face before. Now, you're justifying your actions as if everyone judges you based on your looks."

"I can't escape what I see in the mirror," I rasp.

"Then find someone who sees the person beyond that. That's the kind of woman you need."

"Yeah, well, if you find one, be sure to send her my way," I drawl. Moving away from the window, I make my way over to the crystal bottles of amber liquid on the other side of the room. I toss a few fingers back before declaring, "I'm such a catch, I'm certain they'll be grateful."

Joe is silent for a moment before declaring, "She left not long after you did. Think about that." Then he moves over to the door.

"Wait! What do you mean she left? What happened? I dragged Mel out of there, so I didn't harm anyone."

"I'd rethink exactly what happened, Brett. I heard every word you said to her before you pulled your sister off the dance floor. I'm not surprised Jillian hightailed it out of there." Joe is contemplative before his lips curve slightly. "I think I'm more shocked by what she said before she did."

"And that was?"

He shakes his head. "Find out for yourself, since I believe you owe Ms. Beale an apology."

"For what?" I demand.

"For being a jackass." He steps away from the door and gets right into my face. "You claim you want to move forward, that you're ready to face a fire again, but are you?"

A shiver crawls up my spine at the hardness in Joe's voice. I fling out, "If I'm not ready, then you're sure as hell not."

"Then maybe it's a good thing my father has benched us the last six months."

"What do you mean?" My voice comes out riddled with panic.

"Just . . . never mind. Find the lady. I'm certain you'll be surprised by what she has to say."

After he leaves to head back to the ball, I can't shake loose the feelings Joe stirred up inside of me: primarily anxiety and fear. What if I can't go back to active duty? Will I lose the camaraderie of the men and women I work with?

And what does Jillian Beale have to do with any of it?

I pour myself another glass of whiskey and flop down on the couch to think about what went down tonight. I can't quite keep the image of Jillian's face tipped up to mine, glossy lips parted. "Just as stunned as I was," I murmur.

Using my phone, I quickly search the internet for what business Jillian owns in Collyer. To say I'm surprised is quite an understatement.

"Maybe she won't throw needles at my face if I go to her shop." With that decided, I make my way to my bedroom and pray for a night of halfway decent sleep.

# JILLIAN

"Listen, I know why you bailed on me this morning," Kelsey says as she breezes into Pick the Knits holding a to-go cup from the Coffee Shop.

Even with the short distance between us, I can smell the sweet scent of caramel. Candidly I admit as I reach for the cup she holds, "Because I didn't feel like being talked about any more than I knew I would be?"

Sheepishly she confesses, "Oh, don't worry. There was plenty of talk."

I groan before taking a drink.

"About how good you and Brett looked together. Honest to God, how have we been friends for so long and I never knew you could dance like that?"

The coffee I just drank nearly comes flying out of my mouth, but I swallow it just in time. It sets off rampant coughing that causes Kelsey to rip my drink out of my hand. "What on earth are you talking about? I figured someone would have renamed the breakfast sausage after me or something." Kelsey tilts her head quizzically, so I continue, "So people would enjoy taking their knives to me."

I turn my back on her and resume stocking the yarn into a colorful display.

"Trust me. If anyone is saying anything of the sort, it isn't happening in Ava and Matt's place. Jilly, you were knocked out trying to get back to your grandmother! You were going to die in that fire."

Before I can respond, a male voice interrupts our conversation. "So, that's what happened."

Whirling around, I lock eyes with Brett Stewart. In his hand is a similar cup to the one Kelsey brought me. He steps forward and holds it out to me. "I figured the apology I owe you for last night should come with something. Ava suggested this."

Kelsey mutters under her breath about Ava's meddling. "Not now, Kelsey." *Not when I need to give this man thanks for my life.*

She heeds my unsaid words. "If you're all right, I'll leave you to it."

I step forward and lay a hand on her wrist briefly. "Thank you for caring so much."

Her chest rises and falls. "Call if you need me," she says as she heads toward the door.

I follow her and flip the sign to closed. "This way we won't have anyone intrude," I inform him when Brett raises his brows at what I did. Inhaling the cool air into my lungs, I begin, "I'd like to formally apologize, Captain—"

His brows furrow before he interrupts, "For what? You did nothing wrong."

"For being so foolish to try to get back to my grandmother during the fire. I'm the reason you were injured. I'm sorry, so incredibly sorry, you were hurt in the line of duty."

One heartbeat, then another passes. And something miraculous happens. A smile breaks out across Brett's face that transforms him from the taciturn, yet flirtatious, man of the night before into a charming stranger. I blink over and over as I absorb the difference the broad grin makes to his rough-and-tough appearance. Then, stranger still, he chuckles. He finally says, "You're sorry?"

"Well, yes. I stopped by the station a few times over the past year to make my apologies, but . . ."

"But nothing, Jillian. The fire wasn't your fault, and neither was what happened. I'm the one who owes you an apology for the way I left you on the dance floor."

Recalling the way Brett bristled last night, I choose my words carefully. "Your acceptance is a lovely gesture, but you certainly don't owe me an apology. In fact, it's quite the opposite. I was startled you wanted to dance with me at all."

"Startled? Why?" He moves closer, still holding the coffee he bought for me.

For me.

Why that rattles me so much, I can't explain. It's not as if hundreds of customers haven't dropped treats by in the last year as I healed and opened the store again.

"Well"—I gesture helplessly—"you're you."

"And that makes a difference why?"

*Damn, the beard just makes him even more gorgeous,* I think to myself. I can feel my cheeks start to flush. Something Brett obviously takes note of by the way his eyes narrow. "You haven't answered my question, Jillian," he prods.

"Because I'm not someone a man like you notices! I'm the kind of woman who fades into the background."

Brett cocks his head to the side before asking, "A man like me?"

I enumerate, "You may not believe it, but you're ridiculously handsome. Still. You're smart, loyal, and before I did something to hurt us all, I remember seeing you laugh. A lot." Flinging up my hands, I tack on, "Your sister's behavior didn't surprise me last night. I'm just shocked more people haven't shunned me."

"It was an accident," he declares firmly.

"That's nice of you to say."

"That's the truth." Before I can contradict him that it was my selfishness at being unwilling to let go of my grandmother, he interjects, "You were the first person I saw last night."

"That makes no sense." Brett handed me a glass of champagne. That meant he had to have interacted with at the least a member of the waitstaff.

"You were the first person who stirred something inside me last night," he corrects himself.

My breath becomes suspended somewhere between my lungs and my brain. "Excuse me?"

"You glided into the room, and I became entranced. I asked you to dance because I did more than notice."

With that, Brett lifts my right hand. Unconsciously, I slip it out of his grip and offer him my left. Determinedly, he reaches for my right again. "Maybe somehow I knew we were already mingled, entwined." The fact he's paraphrasing the words of my tattoo makes my heart tremble.

But I want to cry when he lifts it to his lips to kiss because I want to know what his lips feel like—even if just for a brief second. Letting my hand drop, his lips curve before he asserts, "I'll see you soon, Jillian."

Just as he reaches the door, I burst out, "What makes you so sure?"

The look he sends me is so scorching, I feel the heat down to my bones. Quite unlike the last time I was burned by fire. Then Brett slides out of my shop, leaving me to regain my breath.

# JILLIAN

For a year, when I wanted to find him to apologize, I could never locate Brett. Now, he's the first person I bump into everywhere I go: grocery shopping, the Coffee Shop, even the post office. Earlier today, he brushed my left hand when he walked by me. I almost crumbled to the ground when he winked at me, murmuring just my name.

Unable to regain my equilibrium, I leap into my car after dropping off my packages and drive the twisty Berkshire Mountains roads around Collyer. "Is this some new form of torture? Penance?" I demand passionately. There's no one around to answer me but the flashy orange and red-hued leaves. "Great, now I'm talking to the air . . . oh, crap!"

Groaning, I listen to the *thump, thump* sound being made from outside of my car. "That can only mean one thing." I press the brake slowly, knowing if I slam down on it, I could end up spinning out my car. I slap on my hazard lights and pull into the parking lot of a small state park as quickly as possible. Placing the car in park and engaging the emergency brake, I take a moment and lay my forehead against the steering wheel. Fisting my hands as best as I can, I bang them down hard. Pain zings through my left, while I feel a dull ache in my right. "I can't even change the tire on my own."

After a few moments when my self-pity slowly ebbs away, I reach for my cell phone to call to be rescued.

Again.

That's when I let the first tear fall.

About thirty minutes later, a Collyer Fire Department SUV— the initials CFD emblazoned on the doors—pulls into the lot where I've perched on a rock to absorb as much of the serene surroundings as I can. I frown when Brett slides out and heads straight in my direction. "I thought I called for a tow truck?"

His smile isn't nice this time. It's filled with the kind of self-loathing I see on occasion when I look in the mirror. "Who was called to a five-car pileup on the edge of town. Chief asked if I could take a look at your tire."

I scamper down off the rock. "Thanks."

"Not a problem." Before I reach him, Brett turns and heads toward my car. I frown. Gone is affable Brett. "What happened?" I call out.

He pauses and then explains, "Like I said, there's been an accident..."

"I meant with you." His eyes widen fractionally as I approach. "I mean, is it because it's me? That you had to come to help me again? Is that making you feel uncomfortable?" I chew on my lower lip as I wait for his answer.

His hands clench and release at his sides. "No."

"No? Just...no?" I probe.

"That's right."

"I see." And sadness sweeps through me at the realization that I am the cause for his erratic behavior. "Thanks for coming out, Brett, but you can tell Chief Bianco you weren't able to fix the issue and that I need a wrecker. I didn't mean to set off any bad feelings."

He frowns. "I haven't even looked at the car."

I back away toward the rock. "See? No harm, no foul. Thanks for trying to rescue me. Again. Thank you for trying to save me from myself." I turn my back and get maybe three steps when I feel his hand grip my upper arm.

"Listen, Jillian. I don't know what you're going on about. I'm not rescuing you. If you want, I can teach you how to change a flat."

"I know how." God, my voice sounds dead even to my own ears.

His eyes narrow. "Then why did you call in to have your car towed?"

"I—" I start.

"Because it's really not that hard."

"Brett—" I say, only to be interrupted. Again.

"If it's the jack, they even sell an electric scissor one you can keep in the trunk of your car that's rechargeable."

"Goddamn it, Brett. I can't change my own tire because of these!" I fling my hands up into his face. "So, excuse me for feeling a bit out of sorts that the man who saved my life has to be the person who rescues me the first time I find myself in a bind since then."

With that revelation, I whirl around to get away from the handsome firefighter, when my right hand is caught in his. I freeze, completely unable to move, as he smooths his fingers up my hand.

Both sides.

Unable to bear what will inevitably be disgust on his face, I begin struggling in earnest. Twisting, turning, I can't see anything from the tears in my eyes.

That's when he says words that make me question what's real. "So beautiful and remarkably brave. That's what you are, Jillian."

And that's when I fling his own words back at him from the night of the ball with a twist. "There's nothing about me that's beautiful or brave."

His thumb caresses the point where my scars intersect with the healthy skin before it slides down to the palm of my hand. "No? Do you know how you got this particular scar, Jilly?"

His use of my nickname causes my cheeks to warm. I shake my head at the ridiculousness of it all. "Yes, I was burned."

"Sweet, brave, Jilly. There's only one way you got this scar." He traces the almost perfect rectangles before his eyes lift to meet mine. "I didn't save you. I couldn't because you were helping Joe to save me."

"That's impossible," I declare flatly. I yank my hand back and trace over the slightly raised scar.

He steps closer and lifts my right hand until I'm forced to reach around his back. Our faces are perfectly aligned when I gasp as the raised edges of my scar fit over the "F" embossed on the back of his uniform. "Believe me now?" he challenges.

"But, how?" I struggle to absorb this new information.

He shakes his head back and forth, causing our noses to brush against one another. The bristles from his beard scrape against my skin. It's soft yet abrasive. *Just like the man himself.* He admits, "I don't know, but I know someone who can tell us."

I'm about to ask who when his lips curve. From this distance, I can see the way the motion also crinkles the corners of his eyes and the small dimple that hides behind his beard. That's when he declares, "After I fix your car."

My own lips curve hesitantly in return. "I'd appreciate the assistance if it's not too much trouble."

We stand motionless, absorbing the other for another long moment before a male voice breaks through our reverie by barking through the radio pinned to Brett's jacket. He steps away to respond.

I use that moment to regain my bearings. While it's true, I may have accidentally incapacitated the two firemen, apparently I did something to protect Brett. Me. A heady sensation causes me to sway on my feet.

"Whoa. Are you all right?" Brett's face swims in front of me.

I wave off his concern. "Fine. Do you need to go?"

"No. *We* need to fix your tire and head back into town. We have a meeting with the chief."

# BRETT

"She's quite remarkable," Chief comments after Jillian leaves his office.

I agree, but I keep my thoughts to myself. "Why weren't any of us told?"

Chief sits back in his chair and stretches his arms behind his head. "You all had different forms of amnesia about the actual events, Brett. Remember that jackass Emily Freeman-Madison almost married? The one that helped her sister, Corinna?"

I snort. "Who could forget Dr. Dickhead?" Having dated Em for a short time many years ago, the two of us remained friends after she met her now husband, Jake Madison.

"Right. Everyone was so concerned about your head injuries, the Freemans brought him in to consult on the three cases."

My jaw falls open at that news. "Dr. Wheedon never mentioned him consulting on my case!"

Chief snorts. "Get over it. You'd just come out of a drug-induced coma with barely any memory of who your parents were at first."

My cheeks flush. "Right."

"Anyway, your case differed from Joe's, from Jillian's. They advised us that triggering any of your memories about that day could either be like reading you a story or cause damage." Chief looks aggrieved. "Have you any idea what a pain in the ass it was to listen to that blowhard go on and on about the delicacy of the tissue of the human brain?"

I burst into helpless laughter. "I can only imagine."

But my reaction causes Chief to stiffen. I scramble, "Listen, I know it was a tough time for all of you."

"Shut it, Brett." I immediately stop talking. He visibly swallows. "That's the first time in well over a year I've heard you laugh, son."

Now I'm the one with a knot in my throat I can't quite choke down. I finally manage to sputter, "I didn't mean to worry you."

"Both you and Joe did. Every day, I worried I was going to lose you both to something other than the fire." It's then I truly take stock of the haggard expression on Chief's face. It's been there for too long, and I was just too blind to see it. "That girl too."

I frown. "Why?

"Because that's the second time in her life she was caught in a burning building. The first time, it took her parents and her home. That's part of why she's felt such guilt for the last year and has been determined to apologize to you and Joe."

I repeat dumbly, "Her parents? Her home?"

Chief nods. "Jillian Beale escaped the first fire that devastated her life. I'm certain she was determined to protect the people who were trying to save her, even if she happened to die in this one."

I head to the town library after I'm let off my shift. Uncertain where to look, I engage one of the town's librarians for help. Soon, I'm sitting in front of a microfiche machine and the screens are blurring together as they swirl by, but I'm lost in the memory of Chief's words.

*"As best as we can piece together, Jillian, you weren't knocked out due to smoke inhalation but because someone slammed you into a wall."*

*"But how is that possible?"*

*"Because of the way your burns manifested, Jillian." Chief leaned over and lifted her left hand and touched her palm. "Fire didn't cause this, a very hot metal radiator did. With the way the building was going up, it's surprising the burn was only second degree, despite the scar. I just couldn't be one hundred percent certain if it happened before my boys got in there."*

*Her eyes dilated. "The door to the kitchen. Just as I reached it to ask about the smoke, it was flung open."*

*"And then what?" I grated out.*

*"And then . . . nothing. I don't remember anything until I woke up in the hospital."*

But somehow, she helped pull Joe's coat over my gear, permanently branding herself as a heroine in the eyes of the CFD because of it. The *slap, slap* of the microfiche unraveling causes me to curse. "Damn it."

"Let me help you with that, Captain. I believe I know what you're looking for," a voice next to me offers coolly.

I jerk my head to the side and find myself face-to-face with Jillian's friend, the bestselling author Kee Long. "I'd appreciate the assistance."

Within a few moments, she's rewound the tape to the exact article I'm looking for. "How did you know?"

After a few long moments, she pushes back from the chair before leaning over to grab a stack of books and notepads. Her smile is self-deprecating. "I'd be a complete hypocrite if I write about things like pain mingling with a person's Fate and yet didn't do what I could to encourage it." With that, she leaves me to face Jillian's past.

And maybe understand the woman a bit more.

*An electrical fire,* I think grimly. Her mother got Jillian safely out the first-floor window before rushing toward the back of the house to save her husband. At the tender age of five, they sent an orphaned Jillian to live with her grandmother. The same grandmother, I note, who lives in Collyer Court Assisted Living.

My eyes narrow as I read the reporter's quote from five-year-old

Jillian about what happened. " 'The firemen went in to get my mommy and daddy. I really, really appreciate they tried.' God, that reporter should be shot."

"Looking back on it, I agree." Jillian's voice startles me.

# JILLIAN

"I've been thinking since I left Chief's office," I explain to Brett as he holds out a chair for me to sit down at the small intimate table for two right smack dab in the center of Tra Vini.

Instead of being shocked or trying to psychoanalyze me about my past, Brett immediately asked me to dinner once he realized I was behind him. But something inside me is cautious about giving hope more than just a little bit of fuel, despite how attractive I find him. After all, hasn't life proven to me my heart isn't worthy of protection? I'm just growing weary of the number of blows I have to absorb after each disappointment before I'm ready to rise again.

Brett pulls me out of my musings as he slides my chair beneath the table's edge. "What's been on your mind?"

I jerk up my shirt sleeve and hold out my left wrist. Brett takes me up on the offer, grasping it gently before reading out loud, "A man can die but once." He rotates my forearm as he does, slowly letting my hand slide inside of his. "Who said this?"

"Shakespeare. And, boy, was he was wrong."

A hint of wickedness crosses his face when he drawls, "I didn't think we were at the part of our relationship to be discussing 'little deaths,' Jillian."

I take less than a second to put what he said together with what I did. And even as I burst out laughing, I swat at him. "Well played, Captain."

Brett's eyes hold mine for a long moment before he drawls, "Well, I'm no Shakespeare, but I can occasionally put on a good act."

"Please don't." The words slip from my mouth unbidden. The lights dim in the small Italian eatery, the candlelight setting off the emerald tones in Brett's eyes. "Don't act with me. Don't pretend everything's okay when I know—*I know*—it's not. How can it be?"

His breath begins coming in short pants. He slides out of his chair. "If you'll give me a moment?"

I nod helplessly as Brett strides away. He stops our waitress along the way and makes a few gestures. She nods frantically.

Then he walks out the restaurant's front door.

Tears sting my eyes. I reach over and touch my left wrist with my right hand, pressing the raised marks in my palm hard against the inked words. *You're such a fool, Jillian,* I berate myself.

"Ms. Beale? Would you like a drink until Captain Stewart comes back?" the waitress asks, approaching from the side.

"Sure." I don't bother telling her there's no chance of Brett returning. In my head, I'm already making plans to escape. After all, that's what I do best—escape. "I can't even say the right thing to help people."

"Excuse me, ma'am?"

"Sorry. I'm talking to myself. Wine. Montepulciano, please."

"We only sell that by the bottle."

"That's fine." What the hell? Why not have a drink or two? Since Brett drove here, I'll just call for a ride to bring me home.

Endless minutes later, my wine is opened and poured. I close my eyes and lift a glass to my disappearing date. "To your health."

"An excellent thing to toast to," comes Brett's voice from behind me.

I lift the crystal glass filled with blood red liquid and admire it. "This wine must be more potent than I thought since you left."

"No, I went to take a call." Brett's hands brush against my back as his fingers curl against the back of my chair, causing my heart rate to increase.

I twist my head until I can see his face and his anguished expression. "You thought I left?" he asks.

"Right after I said something some might take as intrusive."

Brett holds my gaze when he declares, "I'm not just some people. You'll learn that."

Then he moves back around the table and sits back down across from me.


"Can I ask who called earlier?" I take a bite of cannoli as we begin dessert.

Brett and I exhaust a number of topics over the various dinner courses. We've learned we both enjoy classical music and modern art but consider ourselves Marvel fanatics—something I'm grateful he admitted to since I gushed, "Clint Barton is my favorite Avenger."

Immediately he stopped eating his *penne alla vodka* to inquire with amusement, "Is that because you think the actor's good looking or because of his role in the movies?"

"Well," I hedged.

And he laughed so hard, he dropped his fork against his plate.

Forget regaining feeling in my hand, I'd trade it gladly if I could help bring laughter back to Brett Stewart.

"It was Joe," he informs me.

"Chief or son?"

His teeth flash quickly before he informs me, "Chief. But as soon as I informed him where I was and who I was with, Joe called me. Then the conversation with Joe got interrupted by a call from my parents."

"That many people called you in such a short span of time?" I ask incredulously.

"I had to interrupt Chief by letting him know I was out with you. He, naturally, shouted that to Mama D."

"Naturally," I reiterate.

"Mama D immediately called her son, and then my parents, to inform them of our date."

I flush to the roots of my hair when he uses the word date. "It's not such a big deal."

"To them, it is. You're the first woman I've asked out since everything happened." He drops that bomb as easily as he had dropped his dinner fork earlier.

I stutter. "I ... sorry ... what?"

He levels a steady look at me. "You heard me."

"But why me?" I persist.

His lips curve. "Maybe it's because somehow I knew you wouldn't mind my crush on Natasha Romanov."

I burst into gales of laughter. It takes me a few minutes to get myself under control enough to tell him I get it.

I really do.

After all, heroes are ridiculously appealing.

I should know. I'm entranced by the one sitting across from me.

# JILLIAN

Long after we've finished lingering over coffee, Brett moves behind me to pull out my chair. "As much as I don't want this evening to end, I think they might be giving us a few hints."

"You think? I'm sort of terrified the glares the waitstaff has been giving us for the last twenty minutes might follow me into dreamland tonight."

He leans close to my ear to whisper, "And here I was hoping I'd have that pleasure."

My heart speeds up as his breath tickles the curve of my ear. Then his fingers drag across my back. I try as hard as I can to control my physical reaction to him, but wind up blurting out my thoughts. "Every time you touch me, there's this little ripple."

His hands stay on my shoulders for a moment before they slide away. He walks in front of me without replying. Embarrassed, I duck my head and snatch up my scarf to bury my face in it. "Maybe if I'm lucky, an earthquake will happen right about now. For once, I'd appreciate the chaos that surrounds me being something I can control," I mutter.

"Well, we can talk about that outside, Jillian, but I'll be honest. I'm really interested in that ripple." Brett's voice forces me to lower the soft Merino wool.

My eyes meet his and I relish each and every little sensation that flows through me. Even though he laces his fingers through my right hand to guide me away from the table, and all I can feel is the pressure of his touch, it's knowing it's there that causes goose bumps to spread over the rest of me. As if he knows the pleasure he makes me feel, he tucks me right next to his warmth while he sorts out the bill.

A thought pops into my head. *Maybe I didn't lose one of my senses; maybe I'm just fully embracing the others.* Inhaling, I relish the rich scent of Brett's cologne. I lick my lips and imagine what they would feel if they pressed into his neatly trimmed beard or against his muscled skin. I tip my head back, letting my eyes gorge on the feast of his full lips and high cheekbones. I tune out the hustle and bustle of the restaurant around us and just feel. And when my eyes lock with his, I begin to believe I've been granted the promise of something that far exceeds anything I've ever experienced.

If I likened this emotion to the way yarn entwines itself in my hands, the emotions surging through me are as complicated as a cabled dragon pattern. They're as mysterious as a knit in Celtic Myths. It's Obsession mingled with Venus. And despite the lack of sensation in my right hand, I know what joy I find in these emotions.

I just never thought it would be something that wouldn't be tangible.

"Are you ready?" Brett asks me. His hand glides against the small of my back.

"For what?" The words pop out of my mouth before I can stop them. His lips twitch. I groan. "Well, that was rather presumptuous of me, wasn't it? Forget I asked."

"I don't think I will." My jaw drops as Brett guides me out the door of Tra Vini with a wave to our waitress.

Seconds after we've cleared the restaurant's floor-to-ceiling windows, Brett stops me. Uncertainty and need are mixed clearly on his face. Does my own expression reflect the same back at him as he lifts his hand and brushes my hair back away from my face? "Tell me this is what you want," he rasps.

I hold my breath and count to ten to make certain I'm not dreaming, that I'm not imagining the desire on his face. Then I decide being awake is overrated. Sliding my hands up the heavy weave of his coat, I tip my face up to his in the moonlight. "It has been since the night you asked me to dance."

"Thank God I'm not the only one." His head lowers and he brushes his lips against mine hesitatingly.

A question looking for an answer.

I rise on my toes, fully wrapping my arms around his neck. The soft expulsion of his breath pops against my mouth as he yanks my body against his. He straightens to his full height, almost lifting me off my feet. His lips settle more firmly against mine, which part—just a bit—going crazy for a taste of him.

I'm quickly rewarded when he nips my lower lip causing me to gasp, giving him a greater opening to me, to my secrets.

To the parts of my heart I thought I'd locked up so long ago.

Brett's head tilts and I realize the past kisses I've experienced meant nothing, as his lips immediately send me reeling. He tastes of the dark coffee we drank. I surge up against him for more. His arms band tighter around me and I relish in the weight of their strength.

I slide my hands into the back of his hair. For a moment, I'm pulled from the experience—frustrated I can't feel the heavy silky strands with both hands. That is until he groans. It's then I realize our kiss is more than just what my hands can feel; it's what my heart does. And judging by the way my heart is pounding, our kiss is tactile in ways beyond mere touch.

It's the scent of Brett's cologne as it mingles with the night air.

It's the way he pulls my hair back to drag his teeth down the cord in my neck before plundering my mouth again.

It's the sound of our labored breathing as we fall deeper and deeper into each other.

I realize touch is an element of a kiss, but it's not the only one.

After our lips break apart, the steam from our mingled breath sends up puffs of smoke in the cold autumn air. My lips still pressed against Brett's, I admit, "I felt that kiss in parts of me I didn't even know existed."

That's when I realize there's no better feeling than a smile shared with someone where you can feel every small shift against your own lips.

It's miraculous, just like life.

# JILLIAN

I sweep into Brett's house with bags filled with munchies the minute he opens the door. "I have cheese. I have chips."

"Did you remember the dip?" He lifts the bags from my hands and plants a brief kiss on my lips.

Indignantly, I sputter, "Do I look like an amateur? Of course I remembered the dip. Our goal was to get completely ill on junk food."

"You're the best, Jilly. The last few days have completely sucked."

Brett's been on light duty at the station for the last forty-eight hours, so his comment makes me frown as I follow him into his kitchen. We've been seeing each other exclusively for the last few weeks, but there are still some topics I'm hesitant to bring up first. "Do you want to talk about it?"

He leans forward and braces his arms against the counter before asking, "What was the most frustrating part about your recovery?"

I don't hesitate before giving him my answer. "Not being able to knit."

"Go on," he encourages.

I start to unload shopping bags as I debate some of the problems I had mending not just my hands but my heart and soul. "I went into the store, but it made me feel worse. Here I was surrounded by skeins of yarn I couldn't touch."

And as I say the words, I finally understand his frustration. "You feel like you're not doing enough."

Brett's looking fixedly at me. "No, I know I could be. Physically, I'm probably in better shape than I was before the fire. Something is holding Chief back from reinstating me and Joe to active duty."

"Have you asked him to share what it is?"

He nods. "It's like the goal post keeps moving. Joe's as frustrated as I am. Neither of us can figure out what his dad wants."

I remove the lid from a carton of dip and absentmindedly lick my fingers as I contemplate his situation. Brett's expression changes to something that could easily melt my panties. "Why don't you come over here and let me do that?" His tone is aimed to distract me.

I give him a resolute stare down. "First, because we're discussing something important and second, we have plans."

He snaps his fingers. "That reminds me." Brett moves out of the kitchen and picks up his television remote. A few seconds later, he's queued up an HGTV special that stars my Avenger crush, Hawkeye. My jaw unhinges when he admits, "My sister was talking about this show the other day, so I recorded it. I thought you might want to see it."

Almost in a trance, I move away from our food fest and into his arms. "You're willing to watch this with me?"

He brushes his hand through my hair, sending the shiver only he can cause over my skin. His brows lower. "Why wouldn't I?"

I open and close my mouth before tugging down his head and rewarding his sweetness with the most sincere thank you I can at that moment in time. Even if it means we delay eating for a good while.

I'm curled up against Brett later watching the HGTV special when a familiar song playing during a commercial triggers a thought. "Do you think Chief is trying to protect both of your tomorrows?"

Brett's hand stills from where it had been smoothing up and down over my hip. "What do you mean?"

"I mean, each day we have is a gift. Too easily, it could be swept away from any of us. We, more than most, appreciate that. Maybe Chief's just trying to ensure you get yours."

"Do I look like the kind of man who wants to be protected?" His voice comes out as cool as it was on the dance floor.

"Well . . . no," I admit.

"Damn straight."

"But that doesn't mean that's not what he's feeling," I conclude.

"That's ridiculous."

Stung, I retort, "I don't think so."

"And how well do you know him?" Before I can answer, Brett sets me aside and paces in front of me. "Let me tell you about Chief Joe Bianco. If that man could still be the first man through the door, he would be. For him, fire isn't just an element, it's the only thing that keeps him alive."

"And I strongly disagree. The love and pride for his family—especially for the sons that followed him into the profession—supersedes that. That's what likely fuels him."

"You mean son—singular."

Surging to my feet, I jab a finger in his chest. "What do you call his wife?"

"Mama D. It's because our families are so close." As soon as the words are out of Brett's mouth, his face pales.

I drive my point home. "Do you know what I'd give to have a parent still alive wanting to protect me—biological or not? Yes, I still have my grandmother, but I'm the caretaker in our relationship in so many ways. As it should be. Time passes, Brett. She needs me now, like I needed her then. She took me in when I had no one. But you? You have so much love encapsulating you that you take for granted. Be grateful for it. Who knows how long it might last? Time's one of the most precious things to protect in life. It can slip through your fingers just like that." I snap the fingers of my good hand before I scoop up my jacket.

"Wait, Jilly. Where are you going?" He rushes to stand.

I shrug into my jacket, flipping my hair out of the collar. "To get some air to calm down."

Brett's face relaxes. "I'll just clear the plates and clean up."

"I'll be right back."

Heading straight for the door, I fling it open to find Brett's sister's hand poised to knock. She snarls at the sight of me.

My hands jiggle the keys in my pocket. "Or maybe I'll head home and come back at a later time."

Melissa shoves past me and aligns herself next to her brother. "Yes. Why don't you do just that?"

Grateful my purse is locked safely in the car, I don't bother to respond to her jeer. I call out to Brett over my shoulder, "Give what I said some thought. Call me tomorrow."

"Call you? Why the hell would my brother—"

"Shut up, Melissa!" Brett bellows, interrupting his sister. His chest heaves up and down even as his eyes bore into mine. He steps forward. "I'll absolutely call you tomorrow. Are you free?"

"I have plans already," I inform him, turning up the sweet in my voice to drive his sister batty.

"Can you change them?" he asks, disappointed.

"No." Brett opens his mouth, but I beat him to it. "They're with my grandmother. It's a standing date we have in the afternoon."

"Tomorrow night?" he asks hopefully. Melissa is openly gaping at us.

To not aggravate what is likely to be World War III when I leave, I just smile. "Like I said, call me."

With that, I spin around and head to my car. Once I'm inside, I sit for long moments to calm down because I'm so unsettled. This was not how I expected to leave Brett's tonight, and I certainly don't want to drive on cold New England roads when I'm disconcerted.

None of us needs another tragedy in our lives.

Especially not me.

# BRETT

"What are you doing here?" I demand once Jillian's headlights disappear down the lane.

"I . . ." Melissa stumbles over her words.

"And don't tell me you just happened to drive by." I own acres of property on the edge of Collyer and my house sets back far enough from the road to avoid this very thing from occurring. When I'm home, I want the luxury of being with the people I want when I choose to be with them.

And right now, the woman I want to be with just drove off. I don't even blame her.

Jillian's been living in her own world of hurt. She doesn't need the irrational behavior of my sister interfering with our relationship. *Wait, relationship?* My breath catches when I classify that's what's happening between Jillian and me. It's new and fragile, but it's what we have—a relationship. I take a moment to savor the emotions that flow through me as I purposefully recall her face, even as frustrated as I knew she was when she left my house a few minutes earlier.

Without a word to my sister, I slip my phone from my pocket and my thumbs begin flying. *Sweetheart, text me when you get home. I just want to know you got there safely.* For a moment I debate adding a cutesy emoji to the end, but yeah, the me who would have done that was incinerated.

And somehow I managed to rise up and find another who did the same.

When Fate threw Jillian in my path, she didn't just do so in order to save my life. I'm beginning to believe it was to save my soul. When I'm with her, I can be me, just me—no games, no bullshit. That's what she wants and expects. I can talk to her about things I've never spoken with another person about unless it's the people at the station or my dad. Maybe it's because she's breathed fire and come out the other side tempered steel that's had to bend not break, no matter what.

My lips curve upward when I recall asking why she opened a yarn shop on our last date.

*"Why did you become a fireman?" she threw back tartly. Before I could respond, she plowed on, "Because you have a passion for it. I grew up with a woman who couldn't turn on a computer but could teach me how to knit a two-color brioche with cables." She shrugged as if her words made sense to me until she pointed at the sweater she was wearing.*

*I gaped at her. "You knit that?"*

*"As if I would wear something knit I didn't make myself," she sniffed.*

She doesn't judge me by what I look like because she couldn't care less. To Jillian, the only man that matters is the one beneath the skin. And for such a little thing, she's a damn firecracker. And I can't wait until the day comes when the two of us . . .

"Brett! Are you listening to a word I'm saying?" my sister screeches.

"Do you want the truth?"

"Brett!"

"I know my name, Mel."

With a huff, she stalks around the sofa and drops right into the spot where Jillian was sitting earlier. I scowl.

Melissa notices my reaction immediately. "What? Was *she* sitting here earlier?"

"What is your problem with Jillian?" I shout.

She stares at me like I've grown three heads. "For more than a year, you couldn't remember all the details about the fire. The rest of us were told by Dr. Moser not to push you and Joe—that you'd remember on your own time or you wouldn't. I've had to suppress my anger that . . . that . . ."

"Mel," I warn her.

"That *bitch* is the reason you were burned and now you're dating her? The bigger question is, what is wrong with you?" she screams back.

Jillian's words from earlier flow through my head just as a buzz hits my pants pocket. I lay my hand on it, garnering strength for what I'm about to say. Instead of blasting my sister, something I'm oh so tempted to do, I ask softly, "What if it was Mom and Dad?"

My sister doesn't get it. "What do you mean?"

"What if the fire was at their place in Florida?"

Melissa pales. "Don't say that. Don't ever say that."

Ignoring her, I lay out the scene almost exactly like I now remember it happening. "What if it was Mom who had gone in to make sure Dad was safely out? What if a piece of debris had crashed down and knocked her out? Maybe she was unconscious due to smoke inhalation?"

"She wouldn't do that. She knows better. You, Dad—you both taught us better." Melissa's voice is shaky.

I drill down harder into the story. I have a point to make. "Doesn't matter she's been the wife of a fireman for the last forty-five years— only love matters. Saving that love. That's all she can see. She's desperate, so she charges back inside."

My voice gentles as Melissa begins to shake. "Firemen pull up and ask where they can help. Their chief directs them inside. They do a quick inspection of their gear—after all, they checked it the day before, and the day before that. They put it on and go inside looking for someone. Anyone." I wait a heartbeat. "And that's when I tripped over her."

Melissa makes a whimpering sound. I drop onto the couch next to her. "She was unconscious, Mel. We were readying to move her when the ceiling caved in, and my gear failed. But you know what? Somehow, Joe got his body over mine. He did the absolute worst thing a fireman could do."

"What was that?" Melissa's wiping the tears that are pouring from her face.

"He opened his coat. He tried to protect both of us since mine was failing."

"God," she shudders.

"There's one more thing." I tip my sister's chin up so she can appreciate the fullness of what I'm about to say. "I passed out from the pain by this point. Jillian was in some odd state of half-consciousness. She doesn't remember much. But her hand tells the real story of what happened."

"What do you mean?"

"She helped pull Joe's coat over me." I lean over and press a kiss to my sister's forehead. "Her scars match the back of his coat." Melissa blinks up at me in shock. "Now, if this were firefighters protecting Mom and Dad and their families blamed Mom, how would you feel?"

"Infuriated. Which is how I feel with myself now that I know everything," she says with a hint of shame.

"I like her, Mel," I admit cautiously. My sister's eyes go round before she almost takes me down with the force of her hug.

"God, Brett, I'm sorry. I'm so sorry. I was just trying to . . ."

"Protect me?" I offer, realizing Jillian was right. When people love you, their natural inclination is to help shield you. It's not a weakness, it's something to relish.

Melissa pulls back to say something when my phone rings. I tense up, knowing I put it on silent earlier. That means only one thing: Chief is calling.

Setting my sister back gently, I reach into my pocket and answer. "Yeah, Chief?"

"I hope you were serious about being ready. I have an all-hands-on-deck situation—a three-alarm not far from your house."

I simultaneously feel anticipation and nausea churn through me. Tamping down the nausea, I turn and stride down the hall to jog upstairs toward my bedroom to change clothes. "Text me the address."

"I'll meet you there," Chief says and disconnects.

When I come back downstairs, my sister has already disappeared. I only give a passing thought to why she didn't stay long enough to say goodbye. Then I jump into my SUV and head to the address that pops up in a text.

During the mile-long drive, I try not to piss my pants out of sheer fear of facing the flame-colored bitch who almost took my life. Instead, I desperately try to recall the deep breathing exercises I learned in the few therapy sessions I was provided once I left the hospital.

And I pray.

Because in the end, that's all I can do.

# JILLIAN

The knock at my apartment door makes me believe Brett decided to respond to my text in person after his sister left. I race over, fling it open, and my heart plummets to my feet. Cordially, I ask, "May I help you?"

Melissa Stewart shifts from one foot to the other anxiously and, without meeting my eyes, asks, "May I come in?"

I'm about to open my mouth to decline when she finally lifts her head. Tears are falling down her face. "Brett was called to a fire while I was there."

Without hesitation, I fling my door open wide. "Come in, make yourself comfortable. Would you like something to drink?"

She pauses just after crossing the threshold. "Just like that?"

I shrug. If she knew the emotions that have been ping-ponging inside of me since I got her brother's text beginning with the word "sweetheart," she might not be here.

Then she bursts into my thoughts when she says, "Brett cares for you."

Or maybe she would. I croak out, "He told you that?"

She nods. "Right before Chief called him in."

"It sounds like you two had quite a talk after I left." I gesture her forward into the prewar living room.

"Oh!" Melissa draws out the word. "I love this room. The light is remarkable." She bends over and picks up a pillow I knit the cover for in a combination of cashmere yarn and satin ribbon and brushes her hand over it reverently. "Did you make this?"

I stand beside her and use my left hand to brush over the fine materials. "I did."

"Do you still do work like this? Brett mentioned—" She cuts herself off. "Sorry. That was incredibly rude."

I cock my head to the side. "He told you what happened," I finish for her.

Her head drops, her wavy hair obscuring her face and muffling her words. "At heart, I'm not a cruel person, Jillian."

I sit on the plush sofa where I'd been enjoying a cup of hot cocoa before Melissa's arrival before I say, "You love your family."

Her head snaps back. It's disconcerting to find the eyes of the man I've spent nights dreaming about in the woman before me. "Exactly that. Do you mind if I sit?" She gestures to the opposite sofa.

I wave my hand. "Have at it."

Her legs seem to give out from beneath her as she plops down on the cushion. "I have a feeling it's going to be a long night."

I do too, not because Brett's sister is here, but because of the overwhelming worry surging through me. Then my phone buzzes with an incoming text. I leap for it, ignoring Melissa's curious stare. *I'm glad you're home. I got called in. Just got here. I'm not going to lie—it's a mess.*

I type frantically. *Focus on that. And Brett, be careful. Let me know you're safe.*

I get two words in response. *Will do.* And for the next several hours, as I learn about the love and fear inside Brett's sister—something that causes a longing inside me for something I never knew I wanted—I'd sneak a peek at those two words like they were tomes of epic poetry.

. . .

L ong after Melissa left, both of us sick from the copious amounts of hot chocolate we'd consumed combined with the salty tears we'd shed together, I am still worrying. It's close to two a.m. with still no word from Brett.

News of the fire had reached the Collyer Courant's online news site, including the fact Captains Joe Bianco and Brett Stewart were on the scene. "If I'm a complete wreck, imagine how Joe's family must feel," I agonize as I scan the article for what must be the fifteenth time since they posted it. As I read the comments below the article, part of me wants to scream at the conviction of some comments that neither man—despite their previous bravery, of course—had the mental or physical wherewithal to be back on the job. "You don't know Brett," I hiss fiercely.

*But do you?* The inner voice inside of me asks. Before I can travel down that path, my phone buzzes in my hand. Relief surges through me when I realize it's a text from Brett. Opening the messaging app, I have to blink twice when I read his words.

*Please tell me you're still awake.*

I immediately write back. *I am.*

Within seconds, I receive, *Then please let me in.*

*Where are you?* I type as I fling back the covers.

*Sitting on the floor outside your door* comes through just as I hit the hallway.

I fling open the locks and ask, "How long have you been here, Brett?"

He doesn't say anything. He's just clutching his phone tightly between his large palms. "Brett?"

"I need to make something clear."

Leaving the door open, I crouch down beside him. The stench of fire emanates from him, kicking my memories into overdrive. "What is it?"

"I just want to hold you tonight."

"Why?" I ask softly.

His throat works before he manages to push out, "I thought I remembered how heartless she is. I'd forgotten."

*The fire.* Knowing the scent of cinder on Brett's clothes would singe my memories even though I wasn't anywhere close to the burn, I still slide my arm around his shoulders. He reaches up and grips my nerveless hand. "I work in hell. Tonight I couldn't sleep alone in it." He turns a face so vulnerable up to me, I begin to tremble. "Can I stay?"

Wordlessly, I stand and offer him both of my hands to pull him to his feet before I invite him in my home. I just don't recognize at that moment that by doing so, I'm inviting him into my heart as well. "Guest bath is down the hall."

He closes his eyes wearily before nodding. As he trudges off in that direction, I head toward the kitchen to make a light snack and some more cocoa to bring to bed. It helped one Stewart earlier. Maybe it will help the other, though I doubt it.

Only time heals these kinds of wounds. Then they scar over until they're completely unrecognizable except by someone who also has lived with them.

# BRETT

I luxuriate under the spray of the shower. Looking down at my feet as the suds from the lavender-scented body wash drips off my body, I marvel at being here. Without a single hesitation, Jillian knew I needed not just someone but her. No questions, no doubt. Just acceptance.

A knock comes at the door. "Yeah?" I call out.

"I have something for you to wrap yourself in after you're done," Jillian calls out softly.

My heart thumps madly as I hear the knob twist and the swish of her pants through the curtain separating us. "I'll be down the hall in my room. Take your time."

The door closes behind her swiftly. "With barely a squeak for being in such an old building," I murmur. Bracing my hands against the refurbished subway tile, I try to let the water drown out the images tonight burned into my brain.

And I know there's only one thing that can do that.

I snatch up the shampoo and scrub my hair with the now familiar smell. Frankly, it could be cotton candy scented, and I wouldn't care. It doesn't remind me of the destruction I witnessed tonight. Quickly rinsing, I snag a towel from the rack in front of me to dry off. "I sincerely hope Jillian's not one of those women who has dozens of towels for the sole purpose of decor," I mumble as I rub my body dry with what was an impeccably folded terrycloth. Twisting it around my hips, I fling open the curtain and almost slip when I see what she left draped over the toilet seat.

Wary, just like I was taught to be with fire when I was a child, I reach out to touch the pool of gray neatly folded on the toilet seat. My hands feel like they're brushing through smoke that waifs before the flames burn hot enough to singe, but right now the color soothes. It knits my soul together, to heal what aches so badly. "Have I've ever felt something so soft?" I speculate. And then I realize I have.

Jillian's hand, her cheek. But beyond that, the softest part of her is her heart, yet it's also branded me. I never thought I'd welcome the burn of any kind after tonight, but the prick behind the back of my eyes as I drop the towel and shrug into the caftan is a welcome one. Glancing down, I figure this has to be something Jillian knit to sell in her shop for a woman based on how it hits me at the knees. Fiercely, I decide I don't care. It may be a foolish whimsy, but every stitch touching my bare skin is tantamount to Jillian mending all the hurt I've been carrying around inside me since the fire we were in together.

She gives me hope. If she persevered to create something so beautiful, the man I could become truly is limitless. After I drape the towel back on the rack to dry, I open the door and head down the hall toward the light—toward Jillian.

And when I get there, I lean against the door. I'm a bit taken aback to find her furiously texting. "Anyone I know?"

Startled, she fumbles her phone. Her eyes widen a bit when she gets a good look at me. Then she stutters out, "Mel . . . Melissa."

"My sister?" She nods. I'm floored. If I'd have been given the choice of a million and one names, that's the last one I'd have guessed. "What on earth for?"

"She came over earlier to clear the air between us." Jillian's answer is simple but resolute. She's not going to share what happened between them, but apparently there's a détente in that corner that allows me to release an enormous sigh.

"Thank you for your generosity," I murmur.

Jillian quirks her head to the side in confusion.

I nod toward her phone. Her smile is small, but genuine. Placing her phone aside, she holds out her hand. "I'll tell you about it tomorrow. Tonight, you need to rest."

"I'm not sure that I can. I can't let go of the sight, the scents," I confess.

"That's what I figured." Jillian lifts the lid on a plate of warmed bread and spreadable cheese. Next to it on the tray is a small teapot from which she pours me a mug of steaming hot cocoa. Throwing back the sheets, she pats the side of the bed and says, "Now, before we were so rudely interrupted earlier, you were telling me about Joe's mom. Why don't you tell me about yours? How early did you turn her hair gray?"

Crossing the room, I cup her face in both of my hands. My eyes roam every precious inch of her face, transposing her image into my memory. Then I baldly lie, "My mother is as blonde as Mel is. She doesn't have a gray hair on her head."

Even though Jillian moves away to crawl into the other side of the bed, the sense of peace she leaves me with ricochets inside of me as she drawls, "Right. And what brand of hair color does she use?"

After tonight, I never thought I'd laugh so hard so soon. But after I do, my churning stomach settles enough to reach for the cocoa. And after a few sips, I exclaim, "Damn, this is delicious."

When Jillian replies, "That's what your sister said," I only bobble the cup a small amount when I elbow her and pronounce, "That's so wrong."

But I feel like I have the world in my arms when she lays her head on my shoulder, yawns, and whispers, "You love it."

*No, what I think I'm falling in love with is this, you.* But instead of telling her, I close my eyes and let what's left of the night drag me under.

# JILLIAN

I s it the warmth of his fingers trailing over my stomach that's driving me insane, or the pressure of his lips against my neck? I marvel at the sensations. Either way, I'm in the most glorious dream that I never want to wake from.

"Jilly," his husky voice whispers in my ear before he takes a nip. "Wake up, sweetheart."

"No. Too good of a dream."

His chuckle is laced with a dark need. My eyes pop open to find Brett's hand splayed on the skin exposed between my oversized pajama top and sleep shorts. He's propped up on his elbow, his intense green eyes iridescent in the early morning light. "What time is it?" I whisper.

He smooths my hair away from my face. "Early. I should have let you sleep, but I couldn't since you were curled up next to me. And I . . ."

I lay two fingers over his mouth, stopping the flow of words. "And you need me as much as I need you."

His head drops below his ripped shoulders. Half a breath later, his head lifts and I spy a dark need cross his face. It's something that starts an awareness deep inside of me.

"What will this be like if your kisses send me reeling?" I slide my hands over the smooth cashmere hiding his skin from my seeking fingers.

He aligns his body so he's partially lying across me. "I don't know. I can't wait to find out."

And that's before his lips slant over mine, his tongue pushing past the part in my lips to flick against mine. His kiss consumes my every thought as I submerge back against the pillows to seal this moment into my memory bank.

Sliding his arms in between us, Brett tugs at the caftan. I help him slide it up and over the backs of this thighs and his back before he breaks our kiss to duck his head to pull it over. He flings it off and away. Looking down, my feast of the senses begins. My fingers tighten on his skin. I've never been so grateful for the feeling I retained in my one hand as I drag it over the smooth ball of his shoulder before I reach the rough beard that grows down the side of his neck. "You're beautiful," I tell him.

Brett's hands, which had been frantically unbuttoning my top, still. He parts the two halves and presses a kiss directly over my heart, bringing tears to my eyes. "Not as beautiful as you, Jilly. And nowhere as beautiful as the love we're about to make." Sliding his arms around my back, he lifts my body into a sitting position before dragging the shirt off and whisking away my top.

Wrapping my arms around his neck, I pepper his face with small kisses. My breasts nestle themselves in the hair that's regrown on his chest from where the bandages sat for so many months. The night I first saw him bare-chested, he explained the scars that mar his back on the left side. *"But if it wasn't for Joe, for you, would it have been worse?" He lifted my hand and pressed a firm kiss to the palm.*

*"I don't remember any of that," I told him honestly.*

*"Neither do I, to tell you the truth." He shook his head incredulously at the time. "Just knowing that you would give up so much for somebody like me? It's humbling."*

Now, I'm the one humbled as his lips trace each and every inked line of my tattoo. Brett's eyes don't follow the line of scars on my body, instead following the rise and fall of my chest. "Don't leave me to do it all, Jilly," he pleads as he straightens.

Immediately, I bend forward and press my lips against the side of his neck, just below the line where the hair bisects his scars. I follow the line of his beard around to the other side before taking a small nip at the lobe of his ear. A shiver races over his skin as his lashes fall shut.

His hands roam over my back as my fingers dance over his skin— for him—before my lips follow—for me. First over his broad shoulders, then coasting over his chest. I take my time to absorb Brett in the early morning light, opening all my senses to absorb him into my soul—to imprint me on his.

Brett can take only so much of my exploration. Flipping me to my back, his mouth begins its own investigation after he wages a new war on my mouth, leaving my lips stinging from the kisses. His tongue licks down the side of my neck with a clear path in mind.

My nails clench against his back as I arch into his mouth when his firm lips latch onto my nipple. His fingers pluck at one, and I whimper beneath the pressure of the suction combined with his tongue rolling the tip deep into his mouth. My hips rock into his as I plead, "Don't stop."

Yet, that's just what he does, but only long enough to switch sides. My breath comes out in short pants as each draw from his mouth sends bolts of electricity from my nipple down to my clit. *There must be more than five senses.* The thought is the last coherent one I have as Brett's work-roughened fingers work my sleep shorts off.

Even with my eyes closed from the intense pleasure, all I see is beauty. A hum escapes my throat as Brett kisses his way down the center of my body. He lifts one of my legs and throws it over his shoulder, sending me closer to the edge than I was just a few moments ago. Pressing a kiss along the inside of my thigh, he whispers, "Beautiful."

My legs shake when Brett fits his shoulders between them, and I feel the first touch of his fingers along the seam of my sex. They graze the swollen bud, causing me to tense. But nothing prepares me for when his mouth surrounds my clit at the same moment those thick fingers penetrate my entrance. I thought I knew what the agony of being burned by fire was before. I was wrong. It's nothing in comparison to the climb of completion when you have no sense of when rescue is coming.

I want to beg, to plead for Brett to hurry. But my voice is paralyzed when his eyes stab through me with a blazing hunger. They stare up at me from where he's lapping at the moisture that's saturating his beard. His fingers are moving in and out as his tongue flicks fast, then slow. Fast, then slow. Fast . . .

I detonate, arching my hips in quick succession into his waiting mouth. I feel myself ripple around his fingers as he slowly brings me back down, wiping his mouth with the back of his hand.

I roll into him and murmur that his wallet is on the vanity in the bathroom. "I have your things in the washer in there."

He nuzzles his nose against mine. "I'll be right back." Then he leaves me a puddle of goo in the middle of my bed. I hear the water go on and off quickly, a door open and close, and footsteps. A knee sinks next to me. Brett's smile is the first thing I truly register, and it's right next to my ear. "Sweetheart?"

"Hmm?" I murmur. I really hope he doesn't expect me to be coherent after an orgasm like that.

"Why is there yarn beneath your bathroom sink instead of towels?" His whole body is shaking with suppressed laughter.

I roll into him and find not only is there a broad grin on his face, but he's also donned a condom. Wrapping my legs around his waist, I inform him, "If laughing about my obsession with yarn makes you hard, I'll let you look in my hall closet later."

Reaching down in between us, he aligns the base of his erection up so he can nudge himself inside me. "Later."

My eyes bulge as I feel the crest of his head press in. "Much later."

And with that, our conversation is over as I need my energy to focus on breathing as he pushes the wide head of his cock inside me. Slowly, his hips move back and forth, nudging himself deeper.

Each push and pull drives us deeper toward pleasure and ecstasy, forging bonds between us I never expected. Nothing matters but taking Brett deeper, absorbing him into my skin.

The hard thrust of Brett's hips flings me over the edge a second time. I moan my pleasure. Sweat drips from his forehead as I come down and he continues to thrust. It takes three more powerful lunges until he buries himself tight against my body before I feel him shake as he lets go.

He drops to his forearms and buries his head in the crook of my neck, breathing unevenly. For long moments, my hands slide up and over his back as he presses kisses to the side of my neck.

Finally, he pulls himself out slowly. But he doesn't move away. Instead, he tangles his fingers with mine. Lifting my right hand, he wraps it around his back.

As I drift off for a few moments, my fingers drag up his back until they find the base of his scar—trying to protect him, even in his sleep. The last thing I feel before sleep pulls me under is his lips, placing a gentle kiss on my jaw.

# BRETT

After cleaning up and being informed by Jillian the bath towels are on the right side of the cabinet opposite her yarn stash, I slip back into bed with her and ask her one of two questions that have been nagging at me. "What color are your eyes?"

Instead of getting offended at me, or—God forbid—throwing me out of her bed, Jillian giggles. "I've been waiting for that question."

"You have?" I say a silent prayer.

She bobs her head up and down. "Technically, they're hazel. But honestly, they go from blue to green to gray. It depends on what I'm wearing or even the color of the sky."

I cuddle her close when I admit, "I kind of love that."

"It was really annoying when I was trying to get my driver's license. They almost didn't let me take the test because they said the paperwork on my permit was wrong," she grumbles.

Now, it's my turn to roar with laughter. "Are you kidding?"

"Nope. I had to call Mr. Baker down to the DMV to vouch for me."

"God, was he still teaching driver's ed when you went through school?"

I feel her nod against my chest. "Though I'm fairly certain we traumatized him enough to retire not long after I went through his class."

I shift her so she's looking up at me. "How is it I never met you when my sister went through Collyer?"

She tilts her head to the side. "Quite possibly because your sister is a few years older than me?"

My brows lower into a *V*. "How old are you, anyway?"

She sucker punches me with her right fist. "Damn it, woman. That hurt."

"One of the perks of not having much feeling in my right hand, Brett. I can hit harder, and I only feel pressure."

I tip her chin up and brush a kiss against her lips. "I apologize. That was . . ."

"Rude, Captain. Completely rude. But to answer your indelicate question, I just turned thirty this year."

My jaw completely unhinges. All my insecurities come to the surface. I burst out with, "What the hell could you possibly want with an old guy like me?"

Jillian's face softens. She straddles me and runs her lips up my chest. By the time she reaches my ear to whisper all the things she's been dreaming of doing to my body, I'm already panting. "Absolutely. I'm on board with that."

She sits back on her haunches. "So, what are you going to do about it?"

I flip her over and show her.

Hours later, she crawls back into bed after scrounging up some food in her kitchen. "It's not much," she apologizes. "We may need to order something in."

My eyes quickly catch a bottle of tea that's about to topple over onto the beautiful afghan on her bed. I exclaim, "Watch out!"

"Oh! Thanks. This blanket's pretty old. It was one of the first I ever completed."

My hands brush over the baby-soft yarn. "You made this?"

"My grandmother taught me when I was little. I sell similar ones in the shop." She nods to the floor where the caftan I tossed earlier still lies. "Along with sweaters, robes, things like that."

"Do you teach lessons?" I'm fascinated by the picture of Jillian being taught how to knit and her passing that knowledge down.

"I do, but it requires a lot of patience," she warns.

*It's as addicting as touching her skin,* I think. "Are you working on something now?"

She shifts the tray from her lap to mine, leans over the side of the bed, and lifts a large canvas bag. "I always have one or more projects in here."

"One or more?" I query.

A quick shrug. "I might be working on a pair of socks or mittens. Maybe—like now—a few larger projects. After all, Christmas is coming up soon. I need to not only get my own presents out of the way but build up my stock."

Astonished, I ask, "When do you sleep?"

"Sleep is overrated. Knitting relaxes me without the nightmares."

My hand pauses in its stroking. "You have them too?"

Her body stills. Crap, I didn't mean to admit that. "Yes. I . . . Did I have one last night?"

"No. Did I?" My voice holds a tremendous amount of vulnerability—more than when I slid inside her body for the first time. I fist the soft coverlet.

She shakes her head in the negative. Covering my hand with hers, she suggests, "Maybe a nightmare shared is a nightmare halved."

My hand relaxes beneath hers as I let go, stepping off the path of fear I've been traveling and moving onto the path of life that Jillian Beale chooses every day despite the circumstances thrown at her. "I'm happy to share whatever I have that you want."

Just then, her stomach grumbles. She scrunches her nose before joking, "If you don't hand over some the food you've got on your lap, I might steal it all."

Picking up a piece of pear, I place it against her perfect lips and let her take a bite before I aim the rest toward my own mouth. After we demolish the tray of food, I'm sleepy enough to drift off while Jillian brings the tray back to her kitchen. And I don't worry about having nightmares. Like Jillian said, a nightmare can be halved when it's shared.

A short while later, I wake up to *clickity-clack*. Over and over. My subconscious recognizes the sound on some molecular level. It's soothing because I know what it is. "Jillian, are you knitting in bed?" I mumble into the pillow.

The sound stops before it picks up again. "Brett, are you sleeping in bed?" comes the amused reply.

"That's what I thought." Lightning fast, I reach over and pluck the needles from her hands, getting stabbed in the process. "Christ, how the hell long are these things?"

"I was in the middle of a row!" she yells, as if I've committed a felonious sin. And maybe, in the world of yarn, I have. But in our bed, I need to remind her what its primary functions are.

Making love and sleep. In that order.

Starting right now.

Later, Jillian scolds me about having to undo the row, but she's doing so with a pretty blush to her cheeks while I order delivery Chinese food. When I check my messages from the station, I see I've been told I don't need to come in tonight.

Any other night, I'd be on a rampage. Tonight, catching sight of Jillian curled up on her couch muttering about not dropping a stitch, I'm thrilled. But I know the time is coming when I'm going to have to figure out what my future is when it comes to the CFD.

And it's coming soon.

# BRETT

"Dad," I barely say his name before I'm engulfed in his still massive arms. *Though Frank "Hulk" Stewart didn't get his moniker by the size of his beefy arms that he wrapped around his kids with regularity,* I think with some amusement. It was because when he was livid, his eyes would change from bright green to an electric blue. As Joe and I grew from kids into snot-nosed teenagers pushing boundaries, I had a front row seat to his Bruce Banner transformation. "Maybe that's where my love of the Avengers comes from," I muse.

My father pulls back, studies my face for just a moment before his eyes drift shut, and he murmurs, "Thank God."

My brows lower. "You look like you did when I told you Joe was getting married to Holly."

"Like a miracle's happened?"

I nod.

"Because it has. I have my boy back."

I twist my head aside, trying to hide the emotions rushing through my eyes. "I'm not quite the same, Dad."

"Hell, Brett. Any fool can see that." He loops an arm around my shoulders and guides us toward my sofa. "Now, tell me all about

Jillian. Your sister won't say a damn word other than she's the best thing to ever have happened to you."

I'm astounded. "Mel said that?"

My father frowns. "Why do you seem surprised?"

I quickly catch him up on how Jillian and I met. "Needless to say, Mel wasn't her biggest fan in the beginning."

"No, but your lady appears to have resolved that." My father's face turns thoughtful.

"What is it?" I lean forward and place my elbows on bent knees.

"How do you feel about the job now that you have someone else to worry about coming home to?" He lifts a hand to stay my words. "And before you try to tell me you've always been concerned about coming home to us, save it. I've been where you are, son. There's a difference about being in a committed relationship with someone you love versus the knowledge you want to dive headfirst into the chaos to protect those who have homes, families."

I'm still reeling from the first part of my father's statement. *Someone you love.* "Why didn't I realize I was in love with Jillian before now?" I fumble out the words.

My father pats my arm patronizingly. "You've got a huge heart, but those brains? That might be because I dropped you on your head one too many times. Sorry about that, son."

"Thanks, old man." The two of us are laughing uproariously when the doorbell rings. "That's probably Jilly."

Dad's face cracks into a grin. "Son, give her a key, for Christ's sake."

That's when I smirk. "She has one. She probably can't pull it out." And when I fling open the door, I find I'm right. "Here, give me some of those boxes."

Gratefully, she hands over the piles of gaily wrapped packages. "Thanks. I couldn't reach my key. Those are gifts for your parents and Mel."

I narrow my eyes. "Where's mine?" Jillian has shoved me out of her house every time she's been working on my gift for the last three weeks.

"At my house. Do I look stupid? You'd find a way to open it and rewrap it somehow." Jillian moves into my arms to take the sting out of her words. I bend down to nuzzle her nose. I'm about to lay an enormous welcome kiss on her beneath the mistletoe she hung earlier in the week when a cough from the couch makes her jump from my arms almost a full foot.

"Oh. My. God." She flushes bright red.

"Like I said, son. It must have been dropping you on your head." My father gets to his feet.

"Um, hello." She gives my dad an adorable wave as he ambles over to her. He's a giant next to her petite frame. I merely cross my arms over my chest and wait. As much as there's a pile beneath the tree with her name on them, this—my family—is the biggest gift. As my dad charms Jillian, I wonder how long it will take her to realize I'm laying every piece of my heart out for her to accept or torch. The decision to do either is out of my hands and in hers.

Before Jillian has a chance to recover from my father, the front door bursts open and my mother, Lorraine, exclaims, "Brett, your sister swears that Jillian's here. I can't wait to meet her!"

"Hey, Jilly," Melissa calls out. "What has Dad managed to get you to tell him in the point two five seconds you've been here?"

Jillian appears dazed. "I think I was telling him the secret of how to knit a reverse cable without knotting the yarn."

My dad bumps her elbow. "That you were, Jillian."

Pursing her lips, she eyes my father like he's an alien who stuck a probe inside her head. "My grandmother taught me that. I've never shared it, not even with Brett."

I cross over to her and pull her back into my arms. "It's okay, sweetheart. He has that way about him. You'll get used to it."

She shoots me a terrified look. "I will?"

I nod definitively. "Absolutely."

"But . . ." Jillian trembles in my arms.

I see my father shaking his head and frowning over Jillian's shoulder. My mother's face is wrapped in concern. "But what?"

Jillian breaks away from my arms. Her eyes are wide and terrified.

Her lip quivers as she meets each and every person's gaze, except for mine. "I'm so sorry. I . . . can't. Not again. I hope you enjoy the gifts."

Then she turns around and races out the door.

I immediately begin to charge after her, but when my father blocks the way, I demand furiously, "Let me go, Dad."

"Give her a few, son. Right now, she needs time. And I think you need to explain why your woman became so terrified at the idea of accepting your family."

"It's not you," I defend immediately.

"All right. Then take a deep breath and explain what it is, Brett," my father demands.

I'm not some kid who can be ordered around by his parents. I'm almost forty years old. But my family didn't just simply raise me, they loved me, guided me to become the man I am. They helped me survive and supported me when I thought I wouldn't. They gave me the building blocks to appreciate the woman I fell in love with.

So, I take a deep breath and tell them all about Jillian Beale—the woman I fell in love with and the little girl who lives inside her.


An hour later, my father asks me a question that gives me pause. "Are you going to make that woman send you off to work every single day, knowing you might not come back?" Before I can answer, he holds up his hand to forestall my immediate response. "You're not as young as you used to be, Brett. You've already been injured severely once. Despite what *you're* telling me, I know about the nightmares. I also know that they haven't completely stopped."

"How?" I ask tightly.

He smiles sadly. "Did you think only you were having them at home? Why do you think Chief was so reluctant to let you back on the truck?"

I inhale sharply. "I didn't know."

"No, and neither did Joe. But Holly pushed the issue with him. Now, let me ask you something else. Do you still want to fight fires?"

"I've given—and will continue to give—my life supporting the men and women who step behind the hose. Who pick up the ax."

"That's not what I asked," my father states.

And just like the moment earlier when I realized Jillian was the one meant for me for life, I'm hit by another revelation. My eyes stray to the couch where Jillian asked me, *"Do you think Chief is trying to protect both of your tomorrows?"*

*I do now, sweetheart.* I walk to the door and snatch my keys from the table without another word. Reaching up, I lift my jacket from the coat hanger just as my mother comes out of the kitchen. "Where are you going, Brett?"

"I need to see Joe," I explain. The sense of urgency I feel is unparalleled. More so than getting to Jillian, I need to talk to my best friend.

She opens her mouth, but my father's quiet, "It's all good, Lorrie," stops her protest. She approaches and gives me a swift kiss on the cheek. "Give him, Holly, and the kids my love."

"Will do." Before anyone else can stop me, I duck out the door.

# BRETT

Joe's house is in utter chaos just a few weeks before Christmas. When I pull up, Grace runs around the side yard of their home, pelting her sister with snowballs. Through the window, I spy Joe's youngest dragging a stool over to the pans of banana pudding Holly likely spent all day making to give as gifts to the kids' teachers with a serving spoon in his hand. I snort as he lifts a corner just in time for a head of flame to come in and catch him. "Busted."

"He makes too much noise to be a good crook." Joe's voice is amused. He tosses me a bunch of lights. "Make yourself useful while you're here."

I groan. "Didn't we just do this at my house?"

"That's why you get to return the favor." The two of us make our way over to the half-lit tree in the front yard.

I give it a thorough inspection. "Wait, there are already lights on here. Why are you taking them down? It looked fine just the way it was."

Joe snorts. "I learned something this week from Jason." He names Holly's brother-in-law.

"What's that?"

"Their damn cat hates Christmas lights. Phil refuses to have them up in the house," Joe names Holly's oldest sibling and Jason's husband, who persistently calls the CFD to rescue his cat from the trees around the Freeman farm on a regular basis.

My head whips around so fast, I'm afraid I might wrench my skin graft. "Are you serious?"

"Completely."

"Do we need to get them in every color?"

Joe grins. I blink several times because I realize I haven't seen such an open smile on his face in so long, I forgot what it looks like. "Nope. Why do you think the tree's half done? I had to special order these. They change colors. We can leave them up year round."

I drop the tangle of lights to the side. I drop to my knees and immediately wrap my arms around Joe's legs. "On behalf of the men and women of the CFD, I'd like to nominate you for sainthood."

Joe starts to laugh. Amazing how that sound heals another piece of me I didn't realize was still torn open. "Get up, you ass."

I jump to my feet, snatching the bundle of lights. We don't say anything for a few moments as I begin the laborious process of untangling the Christmas lights Joe plans on stringing in his tree. A tree, I remember with startling clarity, that survived a fire that almost took Holly's life over ten years ago. "We never talked about it," I say quietly.

"Talked about what," he grunts before cursing the packing job of the light company.

"Why you went back in the gear after Holly's fire." Joe stills beside me. I keep going, "Because one taste of it since . . . since . . ."

"Since we were burned? Since you met Jillian?"

My breath rushes out in a fine white mist. "Yeah. Both of those. The need is gone."

Joe tips his head back. "What if there was an alternative?"

"What do you mean?"

He nods toward the lights. "Keep untangling and I'll explain. Pops came to me with a suggestion the other day."

I cock my head, but my hands immediately begin working on the lights. "What was it?"

"Chief."

I mock my friend. "Is the cold getting to you? Yes, you said your dad came to talk with you. What did he say?"

Joe jiggles his end of the lights. "That's what he said, you ass. Do I want to be chief?"

My lips part. "That's perfect."

"I told him no after talking it over with Holly."

"Are you insane?" I ask conversationally and begin climbing one of the two ladders Joe has set up near the tree.

Joe climbs the other. "Not in the slightest. See, through everything that happened with us, I realized there are numerous problems with the support our people get from Victims Assistance if that's all they have to rely upon. My wife's family had the funds to send me to a psychiatrist to get my head on straight once I admitted I needed it, but what about you?"

"What about me?" I ask automatically.

"What did it take for you to pull your head out of your ass, Brett?"

"Love." The answer falls so easily from my lips, I knew it was just waiting to come out. Even if I hadn't admitted it to myself earlier today it would have come out. Now, I just have to tell Jillian.

Joe's face softens. "I figured as much but look at Jillian."

I bristle. "What about her?"

Joe holds up a hand full of lights. "I'm astounded she's found the fortitude to fall in love—especially with you." I'm about to throw Joe's lights at him and tell him to go to hell when he elaborates in such a way, I become a statue. "You represent everything she must fear—family, life, fire."

I recall the way Jillian ran out of my home earlier. "Christ, my father said he dropped me on my head a lot as a baby."

"Then put the pieces together," Joe urges as he begins stringing lights. "Why would I turn down the job as chief?"

I do the same on my side of the tree with the lights. The answer slams into me just as a tree branch recoils, smashing into my head and making me lose my balance. "Shit!" I exclaim as I tumble off the ladder through the night sky.

"Brett!" Joe yells.

I crash down onto the hard packed earth with a groan. Joe scrambles off the ladder quickly. I want to tell him not to hurry. I know what hurts. And unfortunately, it's going to require a cast to fix it.

"Is it bad?" he asks.

"Not as bad as being burned," I tell him honestly.

He makes a face. "Jason or the ER?"

"Can Jason set a bone?"

"Only in the ER after he takes an X-ray."

"Then, yeah, we need the ER." The pain radiating through my left wrist is a familiar agony. I groan as I sit up. "You get to call my folks."

He cringes. "Must I?"

My lips curve up. "It will just be like old days." And, if I take the hint he dropped on me earlier before I fell off a ladder like a damn rookie, an innumerable number of ones in the future. "Have Holly call Jillian. It will scare her less."

"Good idea." Joe helps me to my feet as I cradle my arm to my waist. "Now, let's get you to Greenwich."

A rush of pain hits when I go vertical. "Yeah, let's."

# JILLIAN

I've been with my grandmother for hours trying to find the serenity of knitting, meanwhile cursing myself over the mistake of leaving Brett's house. But it's not every day you see your deepest wish coming true, and it leaves you feeling more vulnerable awake than with the nightmares in sleep. I tried to explain the rush of emotions that surged through me to my grandmother: the nerves, love, and overwhelming fear. Although she's been mainly silent on the issue, my grandmother had one thing to say, "You can't protect yourself from falling in love, Jilly. It doesn't work like that."

Now, as I've been casting off the stitches from the blanket I've been working on for Brett's bed, a bed I've shared with him so many nights since that first time in mine and he drove me to tears describing what it was like for his work-roughened fingers to touch the fine yarn, I know I should just call and apologize. "I was foolish."

"You were scared," my grandmother counters as she finishes knitting a pair of socks for one of the residents in the Vegas Baby yarn she had me buy for her. "She was a former showgirl, Jilly. She'll love it."

I'd burst out laughing at the time she asked for the yarn weeks ago when my life was on the path of love. I'm not even smiling right now.

"I was, am, terrified. Love is terrifying."

"Love is everything," she counters. Setting her own knitting aside, she waits for me to cast off the final stitch before laying her wrinkled hands over mine. "I would have given up my life if I could have brought your parents back to you, my Jilly."

Since it's not the first time she's said those words to me, I can do nothing but whisper, "I know."

She flips my hands over. "And I'd have rather died than seen you harmed by fire again."

"Grandma, no!" I exclaim. "What would I do without you?"

"Grieve. If you won't grieve for everything that's happened to you, then it would give you the chance to grieve for something," she pronounces.

I open my mouth to disagree, but I realize I can't argue with her. "I panicked, Grandma. When I realized the entirety of Brett's family was in the room, I had this realization of the differences between us."

"That's hogwash."

"Is it?" My hands brush over the blanket and I think of the way his fingers dragged along my skin, learning every nook and curve. And the secrets of his that mine will never know. I fist my right hand and feel nothing. "I'm afraid they won't understand me."

"What else?" she urges.

"I'm . . ." And like a dam bursting, it all tumbles out. "I'm petrified of admitting I'm in love with him because what if I'm not meant to have love? What if I fall in love with him and then he's taken from me? What if they all are? How am I supposed to survive that again? I'm not sure if I can."

Exhausted from the outpouring of emotion, I collapse in her arm in tears.

"That's what I've been waiting for," she murmurs against my hair.

I sniffle. I wipe my tears with my sweater sleeve before she scrunches her nose and hands me her handkerchief. I give her a watery giggle. "Thanks."

"I never could convince you to carry one of these," she says resignedly.

More tears flood my eyes when they meet hers. "No, but you gave me so much more."

"Jilly." Just my name is whispered before the vibration of my cell phone interrupts us.

I yank it out of my pocket and hold it up. Brett's name appears. "What should I do?"

She snatches it out of my hands and presses the button to answer the call. I gape at her. "I'm not quite that technology challenged, young lady," she sniffs.

I chuckle before I immediately tell Brett, "I'm sorry. I'm with Grandma. I'll head back soon."

My grandmother nods her approval.

"Jillian?"

I don't recognize the sweetly Southern female voice speaking. Cautiously, I reply, "Yes?"

"This is Holly Freeman-Bianco. Joe's wife?"

"Brett." His name comes fearfully out of my mouth. "What happened?"

"We're at the Greenwich ER. It's nothing . . ."

But I don't hear the rest of what she says. I'm already disconnecting the call after shouting I was on my way. I jump up, saying, "I have to go, Grandma. Brett's in the ER."

"Get going!" She shoos me away before she stops me in my tracks by asking, "What happened?"

"I don't know yet. I don't know if he got called out after I left." The panic that only a woman in love with a fireman can appreciate surges through me, but love him, I do. And it's past time he knows that. "I'll let you know when I can." I quickly fold Brett's blanket and shove it into my knitting bag. I lean over and press my cheek next to hers before whispering, "I love you."

"I love you too, Jilly."

I race over to the door before I take a second to pause. Her hands are wringing together in worry for me, just like they were when she first came to get me when I was five and being treated for smoke inhalation in the hospital after the first fire. "Grandma?" I wait for her eyes to meet mine. "My home wasn't conventional, but I never doubted the love I was given. I only wish my parents had a chance to see to see me grow up before they ran out of time."

"So do I, darling. Now, go to your man. Drive safely."

"I will. I'll call when I know something." I step outside the room but peek back in to find my grandmother using the socks she's knitting to dab her eyes.

As I race to the car with my bag bouncing against my leg, I say a quick prayer that I have the chance to tell the man I love that I'm sorry. And while I'm at it, I let go of the shackles of my past and rise free of the ashes. No one ever said a phoenix's feathers had to be unmarred.

I refuse to fear what the fire can do to me anymore. It's time to for me to face it head on.

I put the car in gear and declare, "This time, you're going to have to get past our love. Together, we're unstoppable."

Then I drive like a bat out of hell to get to Greenwich

.

# JILLIAN

I rush into the ER and breathlessly demand, "Captain Brett Stewart."

"Are you a family member?" the receptionist asks.

I'm about to admit I'm not when that Southern voice says, "She's on the approved list. Jillian Beale."

"Thank you, Mrs. Bianco. Ms. Beale, he's—" the receptionist begins.

"I'll update her on the captain's condition," Holly Freeman-Bianco interrupts. Looping her arm through mine, she guides me away from the melee of people. "Thank you, Azria."

"You're welcome," comes the cheerful reply.

"Mrs. Bianco—" I begin, but I'm cut off.

"Holly," she says in a friendly tone. "I suspect we're going to be spending quite a bit of time with one another."

"Holly," I begin again. "I'd really like to know how Brett is."

"I'm sure. Come with me first and then I'll take you to him," she urges.

Acquiescing, because either the world's about to fall down around me or I'm about to kiss the ground around her in gratitude. I follow her down a short hallway to a private family room. "You know your way around," I remark.

A faint smile appears on her lips. "You have no idea how much time I've had to spend in this hospital between my family, Joe, and our kids. First, let's get that look off your face, Jillian?"

"Yes, Jillian. Well, Jilly to close family and friends," I babble.

"Jillian for now. In time, I'm sure I'll be introduced to Jilly." I find myself oddly touched by her profound statement when I suddenly want to weep uncontrollably at her next words. "Brett's fine, Jillian. He broke both bones in his left forearm while helping Joe hang lights in the tree outside our home a short while ago."

*Didn't he help Joe with that a few weeks ago?* I think to myself. Or I think so until I hear Holly burst into gales of laughter. "You are one hundred percent correct. The reason behind all of this is Joe's stupidity. Actually, it has to do with my brother's cat."

Not comprehending at all, I stare at her blankly until she explains, "Phil, my brother, has a tendency to place his cat in trees so the more attractive members of the CFD will come and rescue it in the summer months. My brother-in-law spilled the beans this week to Joe that Rebel—the cat—hates holiday lights. Joe just dropped a small fortune on the kind that changes colors and can be left up all year."

I press my lips together tightly to restrain my laughter, but a small giggle escapes. Holly joins me. I venture, "Your brother sounds like a character."

"I've had twenty-seven years of his antics. I'm used to them."

"You're twenty-seven? What class did you graduate Collyer" That puts Holly Freeman-Bianco just a few years younger than me. I frown, certain I would remember someone with her gorgeous hair walking through the halls.

She grins. "Thank you for that enormous ego-boosting compliment. Please be certain to mention it to Joe, who, incidentally, is years younger than me. I'm forty-three. My brother, sisters, and I were all adopted. Long story. I actually didn't meet any of them until I was sixteen."

"Wow. That's incredible."

"That's our family. We consider Brett a part of it." At my confusion, she explains, "We tend to 'adopt' people we love into our circle. That's what families are, after all. Just enormous circles of love. We're of the mind it doesn't matter if they're made up of biological relatives or friends."

I blurt out, "I wish I'd met you before I screwed up meeting Brett's parents earlier today."

Compassion crosses her face. She scoots closer before asking, "Want to talk about it?"

Somehow, telling the story a second time is easier than the first. "I've been carrying around this belief I didn't deserve love. That if I loved someone, they'd be taken from me like my parents were. Does that make sense?"

The gold of Holly's eyes flashes. "Yes, it does. What did your grandmother say?"

"That she's been waiting for me to have this breakdown for a long while," I admit.

Holly stands up and asks, Your grandmother is local?" At my nod, Holly declares, "I can't wait to meet her. We'll have to have her out to the farm."

"The farm?" I echo.

Holly waves her hand and moves to the door. "Brett can explain. But speaking of the walking wounded, let's get you back to him. I told him I was coming out to wait for you. He's quite possibly going to yank out his IV soon."

I stop in my tracks. "IV?"

"Just for the pain meds while he's here. He's a stubborn fool. Comes with age. Joe would be the same way." Holly holds the door open for us both to pass through. Turning left instead of right to take us back through the main hallway, we pass by another nurse's desk. "No jailbreak yet, Crystal?" she jokes.

"Not yet, Holly. Brett's threatening it soon if someone named Jilly doesn't show up shortly." The lovely woman turns pleading eyes on me. "Please tell me you're Jilly."

I nod before acknowledging, "I am."

"Praise the Lord. Maybe he will stop arguing long enough so we can spring him," she jokes.

Holly stops outside a door where I can hear male voices yelling the words "Chief" "Assistant" "Are you sure?" The last voice was Brett's, I'd swear my life on it. I'm about to step into the room when I ask, "Where's Mel?"

Crystal compresses her lips together. "Oh, don't worry about Mel. One of the doctors asked her to dinner."

Holly opens her mouth—probably to get the details—just as I push open the door.

And there he is exactly like Holly said he would be—grumpy, annoyed, with an IV sticking out of one arm and a cast on the other. While I lean against the jamb, he jerks his head at Joe and says, "You deserve it as much as I do."

"But I don't want it. This is the path I'm fighting for." Joe grins. "Besides, this way, you have to make the speech at the race every year."

Brett's father turns around to hide his chuckle from his disgruntled son and spots me. "Hey, Jillian," he says. Frank holds out his hand to welcome me into their male-infused powwow.

Brett's head snaps in my direction. "Jilly. You're here," he rasps.

Without looking at him, I can feel Joe's eyes on me as well. I step forward—one, two—and grasp Brett's father's hand. Tears gather in my lashes as I tip my head back and look up into his father's eyes. I see the swirls of blue filtering through the green and blurt out, "Brett, can't you behave in a hospital?"

"Excuse me?" Brett exclaims indignantly.

"I mean, look at your dad. His eyes give it away every time." I flick my free hand up toward Frank's face.

Joe chuckles. "Busted. The Hulk at his finest."

I cut my eyes in his direction. "And you? You swapped out Christmas lights on a freezing cold day so your brother-in-law's cat wouldn't end up in your tree this summer? Couldn't you have waited until, I don't know, spring?"

"Holly spilled the beans obviously," Joe grumbles, glancing over at his wife, who's now lounging in the open doorway.

Brett moans from the bed. I immediately drop his father's hand and race to his side. "What's wrong? Are you in pain?" He nods. "What do you need?"

His hand with the IV snakes up to cup my cheek. "Just this." He pulls my head down until our lips are touching. "I love you, Jilly. Sorry for the audience, but I didn't want to wait another minute to tell you. You're right. Time is too precious. We could waste more of it, but I'd rather the next seconds include you knowing how much you're loved."

I thread the fingers of both hands through Brett's hair, and I'd swear for that moment, I'm given a gift I never expected. I can feel love pulse through the fingertips of both my hands. I whisper, "I love you too. And we'll protect what time we have. Cherish it."

Without taking his lips from mine, he mutters, "Get out." Behind us, I hear the footsteps before the door closes, not to mention the laughter of everyone as they depart.

But I don't care because I'm being singed by the best kind of flame there is.

Love.

If I'm lucky, I just found the eternal flame that won't ever flicker out, no matter what we throw on it.

# BRETT

Christmas morning is riotous, to put it mildly.

There hasn't been a moment's peace since Jillian and her grandmother came through the door. In between my mother feeding us every twelve seconds, my sister waxing poetic about her Christmas Eve date with Dr. Delish, and my father teasing Jillian about the fingerless glove she knit to go over my cast to match my uniform, we haven't had a chance to sit down and hand out a single gift.

And there's a very important one I need to give to Jillian. More importantly, it's time I give it to myself.

Peace.

Finally, my patience breaks, and I bellow, "Presents."

My mother exclaims, "Goodness, Brett. Have a little tact."

My father barks out a laugh from where Jillian's been patiently trying to teach him how to knit. "Yeah, not his strong suit, Lorrie."

Appalled, my mother demands, "What are you making, Frank? Better yet, what are you slaughtering?"

He winks at Jillian, who beams up at him. "A sweater for you."

"No. Just stop. Likely it will unravel the first time I wash it. Leave it to Jilly since she's the knitter in our family." With that, my mother turns to head back into the kitchen for more coffee.

My dad heaves himself up and drops the knitting that immediately unravels. Jillian erupts into a fit of giggles when he says, "Told you I was hopeless, kid."

"That's all right, Frank. We have plenty of time for me to teach you," she reminds him, likely just thinking of the length of time they're here.

His eyes meet mine. I nod, my head jerking toward the boxes. Jillian doesn't notice it because she's fussing over a missed stitch, but my father's face softens before he leans over and presses a kiss to the top of her head. "You're right. We have all the time in the world."

She smiles absentmindedly when he calls out, "Lorrie! Mel! Time for presents."

Not missing the byplay, my mother uses the dishtowel tucked into her apron to wipe her eyes. "Absolutely. Melissa, go refresh everyone's coffee so we can get started. Brett, trash bags?"

"Already done, Ma." I drop into the seat my father vacated and wrap my arm around Jillian's shoulders. She twists herself so she's cradled as close as she can be with the freedom to move. I lean over and whisper in her ear, "Someday, promise me I can hold you just like this until we both fall asleep."

"Does today count as someday?" She turns her head, aiming her beautiful smile in my direction.

Ruefully, I glance down at the cast on my other arm. "It might have to be."

Her expression turns bashful when she admits, "If every day ended with you holding me just like this, I wouldn't need anything else in the world." With that admission, she turns back to finish the row she's working on so she can set her knitting aside.

And I'm flooded with the knowledge she's going to love what's hidden behind the tree.

.  .  .

"Jillian, seriously, stop wasting your time giving Frank lessons," Mom says adamantly as she drapes the shawl Jillian gave her over her shoulders. "This is exquisite. He'll never be able to make something like this."

"I agree." Melissa has put on her new scarf too. Sitting at her feet are the new shams for her bed. "Maybe he can buy you yarn or something."

"He has potential," Jillian protests.

"No, I really don't." My father agrees with the rest of the family. He's admiring the cardigan and matching socks he unwrapped. "What did you do, kid? Pluck from the stock in your store?"

"Oh, no. I actually sold out last week." A hush falls around the room as every person in the room gapes at her. She holds up her hands and admits, "I've been knitting every moment available. I apologize if there are any mistakes."

"There is no way you finished this blanket in a week," I declare, smoothing my hand over the dark gray cashmere.

"Well, no. Not that one." Jillian blushes furiously.

My voice drops so only she can hear me amid the exclamations around the room, her grandmother chiming in, confirming that Jillian's been hard at work on presents. I growl next to her ear, "When did you start this, sweetheart?"

Her lips brush the side of my cheek when she murmurs, "Before we ever met. The morning after we made love for the first time, you took it out of my hands after your power nap. Do you remember?"

"I do."

"I hope you like it."

"I'll treasure it for the rest of our lives," I tell her honestly. Setting it aside, I push to my feet. "And speaking of that, I have one more gift for you."

She falls against the back of the sofa, laughing. "Brett! I don't need anything else. You've spoiled me so much."

I bought Jillian a gift card to the Coffee Shop, some of the moisturizer she uses to keep her repaired skin so soft, a jewelry helper—

so she wouldn't be reliant on me to assist her with putting on her jewelry. But the gift she's wearing is what pushed her off the ledge. Jillian cried when she opened the small velvet box that contained the gold phoenix charm. "We came through the ashes to have a lifetime together, Jilly," I whispered as I fastened the necklace around her neck.

And now I'm about to ensure it.

I walk around to the back of the tree and pull out a small box. Swallowing hard, I stare down at it. My soul settles when I feel the weight in my hands. Clearing my throat, I ask, "May I have your attention, please?"

Everyone stops what they're doing and focuses on me. My father's face is full of such pride, I've never seen the likes of it. My mother's eyes begin to water. Melissa's face is lit with excitement, meaning my parents didn't keep the news to themselves. Jillian's grandmother nods in a sage-like manner, almost as if she's anticipated this moment.

I wish she'd let me know. It could have spared me a broken arm.

Jillian's face is the only one that is full of genuine confusion. Since she came to the hospital and spoke with Holly, the fear disappeared. She's embraced the love I have for her. But now I want to give us the most precious gift I can.

Time.

"I wasted a lot of time trying to go back to the firefighter I was before the fire. In my mind, if I could do that, if I was that strong, there would be nothing I couldn't achieve. I'd be strong enough to work again. I'd smile again. I'd laugh again. Hell, maybe I'd even fall in love. I thought I knew what it was to do all of those things." My eyes meet Jillian's like magnets attracting. "Thank God I failed because I didn't have a damn clue what living was until I met Jillian."

I continue as I pass the box back and forth between my hands. "I thought I was healed, and then I met a woman who taught me the only way to truly heal was to live. She didn't pander to my very healthy ego, nor what I believed she should quite easily see as my disfigurement. She treated me the exact same way she wanted to be treated. And each moment I was with her, I realized I was stronger with her, aching without her. Falling more and more in love. But then, there was my job. I pushed and pushed until they put me back on the truck. Never doubt I loved what I did. Until one night, I couldn't stand it. Maybe I had something to prove and until that moment I hadn't realized how much what happened to me caused something inside me to shift."

Her hand flies to her mouth as I step over piles of presents to stand right in front of her. "Or maybe I'd been changing all along and it was just time."

"Brett, what are you saying?"

I hold out the box to her. "I have a chance to protect something precious and I'm doing it."

"What's that?" She lays her hand on the box but doesn't tug it from me.

"Time."

Jillian's beautiful eyes well with tears as she pulls the elaborately wrapped box from my fingers. She lays it in her lap and drags the fingers of her left hand through the curly ribbons. I kneel before her and tease, "It's not going to bite you."

She lifts her right hand and lays it alongside my jaw. I feel the raised bumps of her scar from where she helped to rescue me against my cheek. As I turn my head to press a kiss to them, she asks seriously, "But will it hurt you? If that's the case, then I don't want it."

Out of the corner of my eye, I see my mother move into my father's arms. Melissa wipes her eyes against her shirtsleeve. And Jillian's grandmother nods her approval. I twist around and order, "Just open the box, Jilly."

Her eyes narrow before she demands, "Is it my gift or not?"

I hedge, "Well . . ."

"Well, what?"

"It's sort of non-refundable." I can't imagine what Chief and Joe would say if I backed out now. Chief, especially, would lose his mind. He's already making plans to buy a condo near my parents.

Jillian frowns, but then unknots the bow. After she tears off the paper and lifts the lid, I hold my breath. She jolts when she realizes she's holding a pin. Lifting it out of the box, she asks, "What's this?"

"It's a five-point bugle star," I inform her quietly.

"I don't know what that means."

Picking it up carefully so the point doesn't poke into her skin, I explain, "It's my new pin."

She shakes her head, confusion marring her lovely face. "Why do you need a new one? Did you lose your old one? And I always thought bugles were a military thing." The fingers of her left hand trace over the five horns embossed on the pin before they gloss over the words Collyer Fire Department. My home when I'm not with her. And as the pin designates, the home I'm now in charge of officially once the swearing in ceremony takes place.

In the end, it was easier than we thought after Chief announced his intention to retire and declared who he wanted his successor to be. Apparently during the time Joe and I'd been recovering, Chief had been laying groundwork under the assumption one of us might want to step back from active duty. He'd been preparing files, performing background checks, and consolidating sit-reps to turn over to the council for approval. Hell, Chief even updated my information to include data about Jillian, much to my shock.

Once Joe made his decision, everything fell into place like 7s on a slot machine. Normally a process that could take months was accomplished in weeks. Chief, Joe, and I approached Collyer's Town Council to ask for funding for an assistant chief position to be created with that role directly in charge of a more robust Victims Assistance Program for both the Collyer Fire and Police Departments.

I was so proud to sit behind my best friend while he stood in front of the council in that closed session. Joe stated, "We're losing too many of our brothers and sisters to the aftereffects of their jobs. We ask them to be our heroes, but we don't give them the tools to regain their superpowers. Take for example, our future chief of the Collyer Fire Department—Brett Stewart. Our insurance covered only ten counseling sessions for him to deal with the mental trauma of being burned. That, in my opinion, is a gross moral oversight. If you expect our people to get back on the streets effectively, then we need to provide for their mental health."

I was grateful to have a cast on since Holly, who had been permitted into the meeting to support her husband, almost clawed it to death. As it was, I used my other hand to squeeze the life out of Chief's hand.

Well, Joe Senior now, I guess. After all, "As of January first, I'm the new fire chief."

Instead of an excited exclamation, her voice is barely audible. "What?"

My fingers graze over each of the bugles as I explain, "There's a lot of things that could go wrong. That's what these bugles mean, you know? Communication. I look at it not just as a promise between myself and those who protect the town of Collyer, but between me and you. And every day, as chief and as the man who loves you, I'll do my best to make certain you all know I've heard you."

Jillian catches my wrist in a death grip before asking, "Brett? Is this what you want?" In her voice is every emotion, ranging from fear to excitement.

I cup her face with my other hand. "I can do exactly what I was born to do. I will continue to give my life supporting the men and women who step behind the hose. Who pick up the ax."

I press the pin against her palm, knowing she can feel the intensity of the emotion surging through me even if she can't feel every nuance of sensation. "Will you be there at the ceremony? Will you be the one to pin it on me?" All around me, everyone collectively holds their breath as they wait for Jillian's answer. No one more so than me.

Even though I already know what she'll say. After all, she's already sacrificed her personal safety for mine.

Tears roll down her cheeks. She doesn't bother to wipe them away when she chokes out, "I'd be honored. I love you, Brett. I'll love you whether you're the first man through the door or if you retire as chief. What job you do doesn't matter, just as long as you come home to me each night."

My head crashes down to hers as I feel something shift inside me as peace settles next to my heart. Being part of a fireman's life isn't easy, whether they're on the front line or supporting those who are. It's an ongoing battle that started as early as the Crusades when fire was first used as a weapon. And soldiers had to be rescued from its effects by their family and friends, who stood by their sides as they tried to complete their missions.

I know I'll find the strength to keep the spirit of my people alive while still fighting with all their might to kill the enemy. I'll find the drive to protect the citizens of Collyer. And I'll love this woman I'm holding until my last call, until the last bell echoes through the streets of Collyer.

"You're certain?" I grit out, my voice jagged.

"I'm so overwhelmed with joy that I can't find the right words."

I yank her to her feet and murmur, "Then show me." Uncaring if both our families are watching.

Jillian pulls my face down to hers and kisses me with every ounce of exuberance she's feeling. When she's done, she whispers, "Later we'll talk about how all this happened, but I'm so proud to be living in a town with you watching out for our safety . . . Chief."

I crush her body to mine and bury my face in her neck. My own tears run unchecked against her neck when I hear her whisper, "We have everything to be grateful for, don't we, Brett? Especially finding each other."

"That we do, sweetheart. That we do," I choke out. I sound like I've just inhaled a houseful of smoke, but it doesn't matter. I can tell Jillian understood me by the way her lips curve against my cheek.

# EPILOGUE

## BRETT

**S**ix Years Later

"*A week later, and residents of Collyer are still stunned by the aftermath of what may be the greatest fire in the town's history that destroyed a multi-generational residence, killing six and hospitalizing two victims. Witnesses who could get close enough to the police barrier to capture footage sent it to CTC4. The shell of the Victorian-style home was still smoking over twenty-four hours later after the Collyer Fire Department deployed every engine to prevent the fire from spreading to neighboring properties. Here's Chief Brett Stewart on scene for those who haven't seen his statement. 'At 7:54 p.m., we received a report about a structure fire at five Holdeck Avenue. Upon arrival, heavy fire had already consumed all the first and most of the second-floor areas. Collyer's crews immediately began to eradicate the fire from the outside, but . . .'*"

Jillian is glued to our television, as they once again show images of my face in the aftermath of the fire on the local news. Her mouth is again moving in silent prayer as the footage a local resident sent to the news station is replayed. Because what happens next is going to be forever burned into her brain, much like it is on my own. Only I was there, as it happened.

I move next to her and lay my head on her shoulder, inhaling the beautiful scent of her skin that hasn't changed in all these years. I don't use words to communicate my appreciation for her support. I unloaded everything they hadn't reported on the news on her the moment she opened her arms the night it occurred. Both of us cried in bed as I struggled to explain what I saw at the scene when I got home in the wee hours of the morning. That is until my wife said, "I know how it feels. I've lived through it, Brett, remember. Sometimes, you forget that."

I shudder against her back. What I manage is the only thing that matters. "I love you, Jillian."

She turns off the volume. I pull back as she does. Her left hand—God, I'm so fucking grateful she can feel the weight of the solid gold band I slid on her finger five years ago—cups the side of my face. "I love you, Brett. Always."

My hand cradles hers against my face. For a few precious uninterrupted moments, I do nothing but replay the last five years of memories as she studies me with her hazel eyes. In my mind, I recall the vision of her walking down the aisle and the sweat on her brow as she pushed out our now four-year-old daughter, Alyssa, then our two-year-old son, Trip—Brett Stewart the Third. My hand ghosts over her hair. "Not quite what we had planned for our anniversary," I mutter. My parents flew up so they could watch the kids and I could take my wife away for a long weekend.

But after this devastation, there's no way I'm leaving my town defenseless, not when it's so vulnerable.

Jillian gets that. She rolls up on her toes and presses her lips against mine. "Your parents are here for a month. Besides, you're needed right here." She gives it a moment's thought before suggesting, "Maybe they should go to Rhode Island instead of us."

"Like you'd trust them to drive all the way there with your babies," I scoff.

She chews on her lip thoughtfully before offering, "We can send them with your sister and Dr. Delish. Your mother needs to nag them about wedding plans."

I burst out laughing, something I hadn't thought I'd be able to do after witnessing what I had and feeling the surge of emotions, knowing almost the exact same thing happened to my Jillian long before I could be the one to save her.

Guiding her out of our family room and back into the chaos of our kitchen, I throw her to the wolves and say, "You suggest it."

Immediately, four pairs of identical green eyes, ranging from my father to my sister and each of our children, turn her way. Jillian shoots me a filthy look. "Why me?" she demands.

"Because . . ." I search for a viable reason. I get more than I ask for when my work phone rings.

Her face softens. She presses her lips to mine. "Go take care of Collyer. I'll protect you from any backlash."

"What's back ass, Mommy?" Trip asks.

My father snorts. Melissa stifles her own laughter. Jillian calmly scoops up our little tank and explains what she actually said. I answer the phone. "Stewart."

It's Joe. "We need you at the hospital."

"Is it Carmichael?" Our newest probie got scalded during the almost futile rescue efforts. I'm already rushing to the drop zone to collect my keys, wallet, and badge.

"No." Then Joe gives me a brief.

My eyes close. *Shit.* Things just got immeasurably worse for the now sole survivor of that fire.

And she's not even six months old.


Six Months Later

"Are you certain this is what you want?" I question Jillian somberly.

She gives me a fulminating glare before turning her back to me and muttering, "How can you possibly ask me that?"

"I just need to make certain, sweetheart." I shove my hand through my hair and peer through the hospital window at the tiny body connected to several tubes and wires lying on the other side. Slipping my arm around her shoulder, I tug Jillian back against me.

"You know what you went through yourself when you woke up—both times."

I feel the small shudder against my side before my wife relaxes fully against me. "Brett, if we don't petition to take her, who will? Who but us understands what it's like to live with the physical and emotional scars of being burned?" Jillian reaches up and captures my hand with her right one. She doesn't think about it anymore. Frankly, neither do I. Our scars are just a part of who we are, what we live with.

Yes, we fell. We were broken, but we rose. And that's what we want to get the little girl behind the glass to do. And we want to help her soar by making her a part of our family since hers died in a fire more than six months ago. The four-alarm blaze that swept through the house leaving her family—grandmother, father, siblings— precious seconds to get out.

Her mother didn't even try. She pitched her daughter's small body out a second-story window.

It was heartbreaking and lifesaving.

The rest of her family died.

And for a long while, due to the internal injuries and burns on her small body, the doctors were skeptical she would survive. Except now she's showing signs of waking up.

Jillian said on one of our many visits, they shouldn't doubt her. "After all, her name is Anastacia. It means resurrection. There's a fighter inside of her. Wait and see."

As usual, my wife was right. And when Anastacia wakes, we'll be here to protect her until she can fly on her own—just like the others who have been burned and lived to tell their tales.

"Then let's see what we have to do." I lean over and kiss the top of Jillian's head before turning her away from Anastacia's window.

"I know what we have to do, Brett. We need to bring that little girl home," she says before she turns in my arms and cries.

"She'll be okay, Aunt Jilly. Dr. Rosenthal is certain of it." We both jerk at the sound of a voice. And that's when we see a familiar face.

"What are you doing up here, Laura?" Jillian steps from my arms to open hers to the beautiful young woman, who's tossing her stethoscope around her neck.

"I finished my MCE rotation early. Then Mama called. She heard from Aunt Holly and Uncle Joe you would be visiting," Laura Lockwood confides. Cassidy and Caleb's oldest daughter is a gorgeous combination of her parents with her mother's vivid eyes and her father's wide smile. Born with Cassidy's calming presence, Caleb's analytical mind, and her uncle's determination, she rushed through her undergraduate work in just over three years, graduating top of her class. Now, in her second year of medical school at Yale University, Laura is part of the elite Medical Coaching Experience, which permits her to see patients with licensed physicians to begin formulating her identity as a future doctor.

If she's as driven as the rest of the Freeman/Lockwood clan, she'll be an exceptional one.

Laura continues, "Dr. Rosenthal was speaking about Anastacia's case in front of all the MCEs. He forewarned us to keep a keen eye on her case, as it's not likely we'll see something like it again in our careers."

"Why's that?" I probe, concerned there might be something else Jillian and I need to be aware of.

But Jillian already knows the answer and says, "Because she's a miracle."

"Yes. She's a medical miracle. You see, Uncle Brett, she never should have survived." Laura cocks her head, her lips curving upward. "It seems to be a family trait."

"Laura," I caution her.

She flaps her hand at me. "Don't worry. I won't tell Mama about what I overheard. She'd have the celebration party scheduled on everyone's calendars before I got home from work. And my future cousin needs a little more time to heal. My guess? Another six months before y'all will be able to bring her home."

Laura kisses the back of her fingers and presses them up against the glass. Then she winks at us with just a touch of her biological uncle's cocky arrogance before sauntering away.

. . .

Laura was right. Six months later, Cia's could finally come home. And she did so as the youngest member of the Stewart family, making our family complete.

Over the years, she's agog that Jillian never cries over her condition—not one single tear despite the number of bandages she changes or how much Cia yells she hates her, me, us, our family. As the scars heal, so does Cia's heart. "Kind of like mine did," Jilly confessed.

After Jillian told me that, I had to step outside to let my own tears flow unchecked.

When she was around six, Jillian pushed her wheelchair for a long walk on our property and told Cia her own story. When she came back, Cia immediately asked if she could learn how to knit. "After all, if Mama's grandma taught her, I think she can teach me," our adopted daughter declared.

That's when my wife teased me, "Brett, they're doing it again."

I groaned. "Stop."

"What? What is what doing, Mama?"

"Your father's eyes are changing color—from green to blue." She reached over her left hand and cupped the side of my face to brush away a stray tear tracking down it. "It only happens when he's really emotional."

"Like, the Hulk?" Cia exclaimed.

Jillian and I burst into laughter hearing my father's nickname when we hadn't shared those stories with Cia yet. "Kind of. Only it never happens when I'm angry. Only when I'm extremely happy," I explained.

"Oh." Cia thought about that for a moment. "That's kind of cool. Your skin doesn't turn blue, does it?"

"Probably not until you start dating," I grumbled.

I'm certain my eyes were bright blue when Cia turned to Jillian and declared, "Mama, do you think I'll really be able to date?"

Jillian leaned over, pressed a kiss to Cia's beautiful cheek and declared, "I'm certain of it. Papa's eyes are just going to have to turn blue."

And they do when I see my little girl wearing a dress in the same shade as my eyes, peering out the living room window, waiting on her prom date—ten years later.

# WHERE TO GET HELP

When I wrote Free to Protect, I wanted to present the point of view of multiple types of victims affected by fire: those caught in the burn and those who love and support them. After all, despite the feelings that might ostracize us in our darkest hours, we truly don't heal alone.

Many foundations that support burn victims and their loved ones exist worldwide. Not only do they support victims but they also offer lessons to their local communities on fire safety, burn prevention and some even offer clinical burn care and research. One such organization is the International Association of Fire Fighters Foundation.

While the mission of your local burn organizations may vary the one common commitment they offer is a helping hand. Who knows? It might be the same hand that assisted with pulling someone out of actual flames.

## COMING SOON

### FREE TO REUNITE

Kelsey Kennedy is renowned for sharing dynamic and life-changing words with the world but when she comes face-to-face with someone from her past, will those words escape her?

Originally released as Easy Reunion, Free to Reunite will be woven into the Amaryllis Series in Summer 2022 with brand new content!

Sign up to be notified when Free to Reunite releases!

# ACKNOWLEDGMENTS

To my husband, to say it's been a difficult year is probably an enormous understatement. All it has done is made my love for you further ignite. Every day, I love you endlessly.

To my son, I love you more. The end. I win. MUAH!

To my mother, I know I turned all of your hair gray. Thank you for always supporting me. I love you.

To my father. You are missed every single day I'm without you.

Tim, I never expected things to end the way they did. I always thought we'd have another chance. For all the times you never heard me say the words, know I love you.

Jen, I love you. Thanks for standing by my side to make it through the internal war I was fighting with myself, then and now.

My Meows, This part never gets easier, loving all of you does. XOXO! My love for you is forever.

To my editor, and my bestie, Missy Borucki. It was like

finding myself in the mirror. Crazy how much we're alike in all the ways that count. Connecticut! XOXO.

To Holly Malgieri - My twin! Thank you for being the amazing person you are every single day and for understanding the crazy (which I try not to put you through). Love you!

My cover and brand designer, Amy Queue of QDesigns, Thank you for calming my panic down and whipping out your magic wand. Love you!

To my team at Foreword PR. There's no way this happens without all of you.

Linda Russell – We might be separated by distance, but not in our hearts. I love you!

To the Musketeers. All for one...here we go. Love you.

Amy Rhodes, you are a miracle of a friend. And thank your neighbor for the use of their cart! XOXO

For my Facebook group — Tracey's Tribe. I'm sending my love to you, always. Now, more so than ever.

To all of the readers and bloggers who read my books, thank you from the bottom of my heart. Thank you for choosing to read my words.

And to anyone I missed who helped me get through writing this story while I was suffering THANK YOU! You know who you are and that my love for you is eternal.

# ABOUT THE AUTHOR

Tracey Jerald knew she was meant to be a writer when she would rewrite the ending of books in her head when she was a young girl growing up in southern Connecticut. It wasn't long before she was typing alternate endings and extended epilogues "just for fun".

After college in Florida, where she obtained a degree in Criminal Justice, Tracey traded the world of law and order for IT. Her work for a world-wide internet startup transferred her to Northern Virginia where she met her husband in what many call their own happily ever after. They have one son.

When she's not busy with her family or writing, Tracey can be found in her home in north Florida drinking coffee, reading, training for a runDisney event, or feeding her addiction to HGTV.

Connect with her on her website (https://www.traceyjerald.com/) for all social media links, bonus scenes, and upcoming news.

Made in the USA
Monee, IL
17 March 2022

92994732R10085